SPECTRUM®

Addition

Grade 1

Published by Spectrum®
an imprint of Carson-Dellosa Publishing
Greensboro, NC

Spectrum®
An imprint of Carson-Dellosa Publishing LLC
P.O. Box 35665
Greensboro, NC 27425 USA

ISBN 978-1-4838-3106-0

01-053167784

Table of Contents Addition

Chapter 1   Addition through 10

Chapter 2   Addition through 20

Chapter 3   Addition Equations and Strategies

Chapter 4   Addition through 100

Check What You Know

Addition through 10

Add.

5	3	1	2	6	4
+ 1	+ 2	+ 1	+ 4	+ 0	+ 1

4	2	3	1	4	1
+ 0	+ 1	+ 0	+ 3	+ 2	+ 2

$0 + 6 =$ _____ $3 + 3 =$ _____ $0 + 4 =$ _____

$3 + 1 =$ _____ $2 + 4 =$ _____ $1 + 5 =$ _____

Solve each problem.

There are 2 .

There are 4 .

How many in all? _____

There are 2 .

3  land.

Add 2 plus 3. _____

Jeff has 4 .

Karen has 1 .

How many in all? _____

There is 1 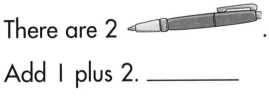.

There are 2 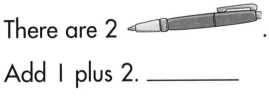.

Add 1 plus 2. _____

NAME _____

Check What You Know

Addition through 10

Add.

9 + 1	2 + 7	6 + 4	0 + 8	5 + 3	1 + 6
4 + 4	0 + 9	3 + 6	2 + 8	7 + 3	3 + 4
10 + 0	1 + 4	2 + 5	8 + 1	5 + 5	6 + 2

Solve each problem.

There are 4 .

5 more come.

Now how
many are here? _____

There are 7 in a tree.

3 climb up.

How many in all? _____

Jenny has 5 .

She finds 2 more .

What is the
sum of 5 plus 2? _____

I buy 4 ✏ on Monday.

I buy 6 ✏ on Friday.

How many did
I buy in all? _____

Lesson 1.1 Adding through 3

Add.

$1 + 1 =$ _____ 2

one plus one equals two

$\begin{array}{r} 1 \\ + 1 \\ \hline 2 \end{array}$

$2 + 1 =$ _____

$\begin{array}{r} 2 \\ + 1 \\ \hline \end{array}$

$1 + 2 =$ _____

$\begin{array}{r} 1 \\ + 2 \\ \hline \end{array}$

$1 + 0 =$ _____

$\begin{array}{r} 1 \\ + 0 \\ \hline \end{array}$

$2 + 0 =$ _____

$\begin{array}{r} 2 \\ + 0 \\ \hline \end{array}$

$0 + 1 =$ _____

$\begin{array}{r} 0 \\ + 1 \\ \hline \end{array}$

$0 + 2 =$ _____

$\begin{array}{r} 0 \\ + 2 \\ \hline \end{array}$

$3 + 0 =$ _____

$\begin{array}{r} 3 \\ + 0 \\ \hline \end{array}$

$0 + 0 =$ _____

$\begin{array}{r} 0 \\ + 0 \\ \hline \end{array}$

$0 + 3 =$ _____

$\begin{array}{r} 0 \\ + 3 \\ \hline \end{array}$

Lesson 1.2 Adding to 4 and 5

Add.

$2 + 3 =$ _____ 5

$$\begin{array}{r} 2 \\ + 3 \\ \hline \end{array}$$

$2 + 2 =$ _____

$$\begin{array}{r} 2 \\ + 2 \\ \hline \end{array}$$

$3 + 2 =$ _____

$$\begin{array}{r} 3 \\ + 2 \\ \hline \end{array}$$

$1 + 3 =$ _____

$$\begin{array}{r} 1 \\ + 3 \\ \hline \end{array}$$

$5 + 0 =$ _____

$$\begin{array}{r} 5 \\ + 0 \\ \hline \end{array}$$

$3 + 1 =$ _____

$$\begin{array}{r} 3 \\ + 1 \\ \hline \end{array}$$

$0 + 5 =$ _____

$$\begin{array}{r} 0 \\ + 5 \\ \hline \end{array}$$

$0 + 4 =$ _____

$$\begin{array}{r} 0 \\ + 4 \\ \hline \end{array}$$

$4 + 1 =$ _____

$$\begin{array}{r} 4 \\ + 1 \\ \hline \end{array}$$

$4 + 0 =$ _____

$$\begin{array}{r} 4 \\ + 0 \\ \hline \end{array}$$

$1 + 4 =$ _____

$$\begin{array}{r} 1 \\ + 4 \\ \hline \end{array}$$

Lesson 1.3 Adding to 6

Add.

$4 + 2 = \underline{}$
$\begin{array}{r} 4 \\ + 2 \\ \hline \end{array}$

$5 + 1 = \underline{}$
$\begin{array}{r} 5 \\ + 1 \\ \hline \end{array}$

$2 + 4 = \underline{}$
$\begin{array}{r} 2 \\ + 4 \\ \hline \end{array}$

$1 + 5 = \underline{}$
$\begin{array}{r} 1 \\ + 5 \\ \hline \end{array}$

$6 + 0 = \underline{}$
$\begin{array}{r} 6 \\ + 0 \\ \hline \end{array}$

$3 + 3 = \underline{}$
$\begin{array}{r} 3 \\ + 3 \\ \hline \end{array}$

$0 + 6 = \underline{}$
$\begin{array}{r} 0 \\ + 6 \\ \hline \end{array}$

$\begin{array}{r} 3 \\ + 3 \\ \hline \end{array}$
$\begin{array}{r} 4 \\ + 2 \\ \hline \end{array}$
$\begin{array}{r} 6 \\ + 0 \\ \hline \end{array}$
$\begin{array}{r} 5 \\ + 1 \\ \hline \end{array}$
$\begin{array}{r} 0 \\ + 6 \\ \hline \end{array}$
$\begin{array}{r} 1 \\ + 5 \\ \hline \end{array}$

$4 + 2 = \underline{}$ $1 + 5 = \underline{}$ $3 + 3 = \underline{}$

$6 + 0 = \underline{}$ $2 + 4 = \underline{}$ $5 + 1 = \underline{}$

Lesson 1.4 Addition Facts 0–6

Add.

| $\begin{array}{r} 2 \\ +3 \\ \hline 5 \end{array}$ | $\begin{array}{r} 3 \\ +2 \\ \hline 5 \end{array}$ | $\begin{array}{r} 5 \\ +1 \\ \hline \end{array}$ | $\begin{array}{r} 1 \\ +5 \\ \hline \end{array}$ | $\begin{array}{r} 2 \\ +4 \\ \hline \end{array}$ | $\begin{array}{r} 4 \\ +2 \\ \hline \end{array}$ |

3 + 1 = _____

1 + 3 = _____

3 + 3 = _____

$\begin{array}{r} 1 \\ +1 \\ \hline \end{array}$

| $\begin{array}{r} 1 \\ +2 \\ \hline \end{array}$ | $\begin{array}{r} 2 \\ +1 \\ \hline \end{array}$ | $\begin{array}{r} 4 \\ +0 \\ \hline \end{array}$ | $\begin{array}{r} 0 \\ +4 \\ \hline \end{array}$ |

2 + 0 = _____

0 + 2 = _____

| $\begin{array}{r} 2 \\ +2 \\ \hline \end{array}$ | $\begin{array}{r} 4 \\ +1 \\ \hline \end{array}$ | $\begin{array}{r} 1 \\ +4 \\ \hline \end{array}$ |

5 + 0 = _____

0 + 5 = _____

Lesson 1.5 Problem Solving

Solve each problem.

Betsy has 5 🌼.

Drew has 1 🌼.

Add 5 plus 1. _____

$$\begin{array}{r} 5 \\ + 1 \\ \hline 6 \end{array}$$

Eric saw 2 🏠.

Esther saw 4 🏠.

How many in all? _____

The farmer has 3 🐐.

The farmer gets 3 more 🐐.

How many does the farmer have now? _____

There are 3 🍁 on the ground.

1 more 🍁 falls to the ground.

What is 3 + 1? _____

Fuji has 2 🤸.

Steve has 1 🤸.

What is the sum? _____

There are 2 🐓.

Then 3 more 🐓 come.

What is 2 plus 3? _____

Lesson 1.5 Problem Solving

Solve each problem.

Ella has 1 .

Carlos has 1 .

What is the sum? ____2____

$$\begin{array}{r} 1 \\ +\ 1 \\ \hline 2 \end{array}$$

I have 1 .

I buy 4 .

What is 1 plus 4? _____

Len has 2 🪙.

Tami has 4 🪙.

How many in all? _____

4  are flying.

2 ✈ take off. # land on

How many are flying now? ____6____

Will picked 2 🍑.

Nita picked 3 🍑.

Add 2 + 3. _____

I found 6  in the drawer.

I found 0 ✏ on the desk.

How many did I find? _____

Lesson 1.6 Adding to 7

Add.

$5 + 2 = \underline{\quad 7 \quad}$

$\begin{array}{r} 5 \\ + 2 \\ \hline 7 \end{array}$

$3 + 4 = \underline{\qquad}$

$\begin{array}{r} 3 \\ + 4 \\ \hline \end{array}$

$2 + 5 = \underline{\qquad}$

$\begin{array}{r} 2 \\ + 5 \\ \hline \end{array}$

$4 + 3 = \underline{\qquad}$

$\begin{array}{r} 4 \\ + 3 \\ \hline \end{array}$

$6 + 1 = \underline{\qquad}$

$\begin{array}{r} 6 \\ + 1 \\ \hline \end{array}$

$7 + 0 = \underline{\qquad}$

$\begin{array}{r} 7 \\ + 0 \\ \hline \end{array}$

$1 + 6 = \underline{\qquad}$

$\begin{array}{r} 1 \\ + 6 \\ \hline \end{array}$

$0 + 7 = \underline{\qquad}$

$\begin{array}{r} 0 \\ + 7 \\ \hline \end{array}$

$\begin{array}{r} 3 \\ + 4 \\ \hline \end{array}$ $\qquad$ $\begin{array}{r} 2 \\ + 5 \\ \hline \end{array}$ $\qquad$ $\begin{array}{r} 6 \\ + 1 \\ \hline \end{array}$ $\qquad$ $\begin{array}{r} 0 \\ + 7 \\ \hline \end{array}$ $\qquad$ $\begin{array}{r} 1 \\ + 6 \\ \hline \end{array}$ $\qquad$ $\begin{array}{r} 5 \\ + 2 \\ \hline \end{array}$

Lesson 1.7 Adding to 8

Add.

$3 + 5 =$ _____ 8

$$\begin{array}{r} 3 \\ + 5 \\ \hline 8 \end{array}$$

$2 + 6 =$ _____

$$\begin{array}{r} 2 \\ + 6 \\ \hline \end{array}$$

$5 + 3 =$ _____

$$\begin{array}{r} 5 \\ + 3 \\ \hline \end{array}$$

$6 + 2 =$ _____

$$\begin{array}{r} 6 \\ + 2 \\ \hline \end{array}$$

$8 + 0 =$ _____

$$\begin{array}{r} 8 \\ + 0 \\ \hline \end{array}$$

$4 + 4 =$ _____

$$\begin{array}{r} 4 \\ + 4 \\ \hline \end{array}$$

$0 + 8 =$ _____

$$\begin{array}{r} 0 \\ + 8 \\ \hline \end{array}$$

$$\begin{array}{r} 4 \\ + 4 \\ \hline \end{array} \qquad \begin{array}{r} 2 \\ + 6 \\ \hline \end{array} \qquad \begin{array}{r} 1 \\ + 7 \\ \hline \end{array} \qquad \begin{array}{r} 8 \\ + 0 \\ \hline \end{array} \qquad \begin{array}{r} 6 \\ + 2 \\ \hline \end{array} \qquad \begin{array}{r} 5 \\ + 3 \\ \hline \end{array}$$

Lesson 1.8 Adding to 9

Add.

3 + 6 = _____

$\begin{array}{r} 3 \\ + 6 \\ \hline \end{array}$

1 + 8 = _____

$\begin{array}{r} 1 \\ + 8 \\ \hline \end{array}$

6 + 3 = _____

$\begin{array}{r} 6 \\ + 3 \\ \hline \end{array}$

8 + 1 = _____

$\begin{array}{r} 8 \\ + 1 \\ \hline \end{array}$

9 + 0 = _____

$\begin{array}{r} 9 \\ + 0 \\ \hline \end{array}$

5 + 4 = _____

$\begin{array}{r} 5 \\ + 4 \\ \hline \end{array}$

0 + 9 = _____

$\begin{array}{r} 0 \\ + 9 \\ \hline \end{array}$

4 + 5 = _____

$\begin{array}{r} 4 \\ + 5 \\ \hline \end{array}$

2 + 7 = _____

$\begin{array}{r} 2 \\ + 7 \\ \hline \end{array}$

7 + 2 = _____

$\begin{array}{r} 7 \\ + 2 \\ \hline \end{array}$

$\begin{array}{r} 4 \\ + 5 \\ \hline \end{array}$
$\begin{array}{r} 2 \\ + 7 \\ \hline \end{array}$
$\begin{array}{r} 0 \\ + 9 \\ \hline \end{array}$
$\begin{array}{r} 6 \\ + 3 \\ \hline \end{array}$
$\begin{array}{r} 7 \\ + 2 \\ \hline \end{array}$
$\begin{array}{r} 1 \\ + 8 \\ \hline \end{array}$

Lesson 1.9 Adding to 10

Add.

$4 + 6 =$ _____ 10

$$\begin{array}{r} 4 \\ + 6 \\ \hline 10 \end{array}$$

$8 + 2 =$ _____

$$\begin{array}{r} 8 \\ + 2 \\ \hline \end{array}$$

$6 + 4 =$ _____

$$\begin{array}{r} 6 \\ + 4 \\ \hline \end{array}$$

$2 + 8 =$ _____

$$\begin{array}{r} 2 \\ + 8 \\ \hline \end{array}$$

$1 + 9 =$ _____

$$\begin{array}{r} 1 \\ + 9 \\ \hline \end{array}$$

$3 + 7 =$ _____

$$\begin{array}{r} 3 \\ + 7 \\ \hline \end{array}$$

$9 + 1 =$ _____

$$\begin{array}{r} 9 \\ + 1 \\ \hline \end{array}$$

$7 + 3 =$ _____

$$\begin{array}{r} 7 \\ + 3 \\ \hline \end{array}$$

$$\begin{array}{r} 4 \\ + 6 \\ \hline \end{array} \qquad \begin{array}{r} 5 \\ + 5 \\ \hline \end{array} \qquad \begin{array}{r} 10 \\ + 0 \\ \hline \end{array} \qquad \begin{array}{r} 3 \\ + 7 \\ \hline \end{array} \qquad \begin{array}{r} 8 \\ + 2 \\ \hline \end{array} \qquad \begin{array}{r} 9 \\ + 1 \\ \hline \end{array}$$

Lesson 1.10 Addition Facts 7–10

Add.

4	5		3	7		4	6
+ 5	+ 4		+ 7	+ 3		+ 6	+ 4
9	9						

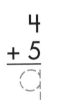

5 + 2 = _____   6 + 3 = _____   4
                                     + 4
2 + 5 = _____   3 + 6 = _____

1	7		5			8	1
+ 7	+ 1		+ 5			+ 1	+ 8

4	3		2	6		7	0
+ 3	+ 4		+ 6	+ 2		+ 0	+ 7

Lesson 1.11 Addition Practice through 10

Add.

3 + 5 8	1 + 8	7 + 2	4 + 6	4 + 4	2 + 5
4 + 5	3 + 4	9 + 1	0 + 10	6 + 3	3 + 7
8 + 0	3 + 7	0 + 7	6 + 2	7 + 3	0 + 9
6 + 1	5 + 2	8 + 2	5 + 5	4 + 3	2 + 7
9 + 0	6 + 4	1 + 6	3 + 0	2 + 8	5 + 3
5 + 4	2 + 4	7 + 0	8 + 1	10 + 0	1 + 2

NAME _____

Lesson 1.12 Problem Solving

Solve each problem.

There are 8 .

There are 2 .

What is the sum? __10__

$$\begin{array}{r} 8 \\ + 2 \\ \hline 10 \end{array}$$

There are 6 🦛.

3 more 🦛 come.

What is 6 plus 3? _____

I have 4 ✏.

I buy 4 more ✏.

How many do I have now? _____

Ivan has 2 🦕.

Helen has 5 🦕.

What is 2 + 5? _____

There are 7 🐦.

3 more 🐦 come.

How many in all? _____

Spectrum Addition
Grade 1

Chapter 1, Lesson 12
Addition through 10
19

Lesson 1.12 Problem Solving

SHOW YOUR WORK

Solve each problem.

6 are on the ramp.

3 are on the bridge.

How many cars in all? ____9____

$$\begin{array}{r} 6 \\ + 3 \\ \hline 9 \end{array}$$

Ines buys 1 .

She buys 4 🐛.

How many toys does she buy? _____

Jordan has 3 🎈.

He has 5 🎈.

How many balloons in all? _____

3 kids drink 🧃.

2 kids drink .

What is the sum of 3 plus 2? _____

Victor used 4 ✏️ in March.

He used 2 ✏️ in April.

How many did he use in all? _____

Lin buys 4 🍑.

Barb buys 4 🍎.

How many fruits do they buy? _____

Check What You Learned

Addition through 10

Add.

4 + 1	5 + 1	3 + 2	2 + 4	3 + 0	1 + 3
0 + 6	3 + 1	2 + 2	1 + 0	3 + 3	2 + 3
4 + 0	1 + 2	0 + 5	1 + 1	4 + 2	6 + 0

CHAPTER 1 POSTTEST

Solve each problem.

There are 2 .

Then 3 more  come.

Add to find the sum. _____

There are 6 🦛.

1 🦛 joins the group.

What is 6 plus 1? _____

I have 3 🎩.

I buy 3 more .

What is 3 plus 3? _____

There are 3 🛶.

Then, 1 more 🛶 comes.

How many in all? _____

Check What You Learned

Addition through 10

Add.

4	0	2	8	5	1
+ 5	+ 7	+ 6	+ 2	+ 5	+ 8

7	1	3	6	8	3
+ 2	+ 9	+ 5	+ 1	+ 0	+ 7

6	4	5	10	7	4
+ 3	+ 4	+ 2	+ 0	+ 1	+ 3

Solve each problem.

There are 8 .

There are 2 .

How many
animals in all? _____

9 were used to make bread.

1 was used in a smoothie.

How many
bananas were used? _____

Dan buys 5 .

He buys 3 .

How many
toys does he buy? _____

There are 4 🐦.

3 more 🐦 come.

What is the sum? _____

Check What You Know

Addition through 20

Add.

5	9	8	6	4	7
+ 6	+ 9	+ 7	+ 8	+ 9	+ 5

8	8	7	8	6	7
+ 9	+ 8	+ 9	+ 5	+ 6	+ 4

9	7	7	11	12	11
+ 6	+ 6	+ 7	+ 8	+ 9	+ 9

Solve each problem.

There are 8 in a jar.

There are 9 on the table.

How many
 in all? _____

There are 11 in the bag.

The coach adds 9 .

How many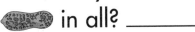
are in the bag? _____

12 hide behind a rock.

6 more hide.

How many
 are hiding? _____

There are 6 .

There are 8 .

How many
shoes in all? _____

Lesson 2.1 Counting On from 10

Count on from 10. Write a number in each blank.

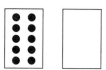 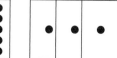

$10 + \underline{} = \underline{}$

$10 + \underline{} = \underline{}$

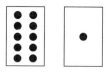

$10 + \underline{} = \underline{}$

 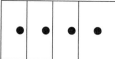

$10 + \underline{} = \underline{}$

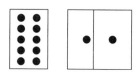

$10 + \underline{} = \underline{}$

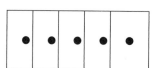

$10 + \underline{} = \underline{}$

Lesson 2.1 Counting On from 10

Count on from 10. Write a number in each blank.

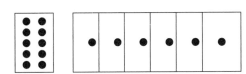   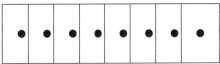

10 + _____ = _____   10 + _____ = _____

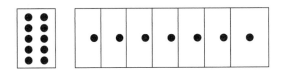   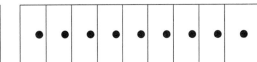

10 + _____ = _____   10 + _____ = _____

10 + _____ = _____

Lesson 2.2 Adding to 11

Add.

$$\begin{array}{r} 7 \\ + 4 \\ \hline \end{array}$$

$$\begin{array}{r} 8 \\ + 3 \\ \hline \end{array}$$

$$\begin{array}{r} 6 \\ + 5 \\ \hline \end{array}$$

$$\begin{array}{r} 9 \\ + 2 \\ \hline \end{array}$$

$$\begin{array}{r} 4 \\ + 7 \\ \hline \end{array}$$

$$\begin{array}{r} 3 \\ + 8 \\ \hline \end{array}$$

$$\begin{array}{r} 5 \\ + 6 \\ \hline \end{array}$$

$$\begin{array}{r} 2 \\ + 9 \\ \hline \end{array}$$

$$\begin{array}{r} 5 \\ + 6 \\ \hline \end{array} \qquad \begin{array}{r} 10 \\ + 1 \\ \hline \end{array} \qquad \begin{array}{r} 4 \\ + 7 \\ \hline \end{array} \qquad \begin{array}{r} 2 \\ + 9 \\ \hline \end{array} \qquad \begin{array}{r} 6 \\ + 5 \\ \hline \end{array} \qquad \begin{array}{r} 8 \\ + 3 \\ \hline \end{array}$$

Lesson 2.3 Adding to 12

Add.

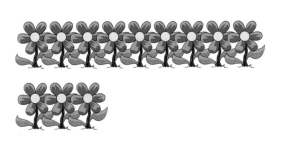
$$\begin{array}{r} 9 \\ + 3 \\ \hline 12 \end{array}$$

$$\begin{array}{r} 3 \\ + 9 \\ \hline \end{array}$$

$$\begin{array}{r} 4 \\ + 8 \\ \hline \end{array}$$

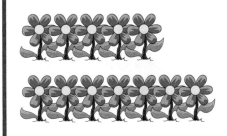
$$\begin{array}{r} 5 \\ + 7 \\ \hline \end{array}$$

$$\begin{array}{r} 7 \\ + 5 \\ \hline \end{array}$$

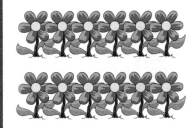
$$\begin{array}{r} 6 \\ + 6 \\ \hline \end{array}$$

$$\begin{array}{r} 5 \\ + 7 \\ \hline \end{array} \qquad \begin{array}{r} 8 \\ + 4 \\ \hline \end{array} \qquad \begin{array}{r} 9 \\ + 3 \\ \hline \end{array} \qquad \begin{array}{r} 6 \\ + 6 \\ \hline \end{array} \qquad \begin{array}{r} 10 \\ + 2 \\ \hline \end{array} \qquad \begin{array}{r} 7 \\ + 5 \\ \hline \end{array}$$

$2 + 10 = \underline{\hspace{1.5cm}}$ $8 + 4 = \underline{\hspace{1.5cm}}$ $6 + 6 = \underline{\hspace{1.5cm}}$

$9 + 3 = \underline{\hspace{1.5cm}}$ $7 + 5 = \underline{\hspace{1.5cm}}$ $3 + 9 = \underline{\hspace{1.5cm}}$

NAME _____

Lesson 2.4 Adding to 13

Add.

$$\begin{array}{r} 6 \\ + 7 \\ \hline 13 \end{array}$$

$$\begin{array}{r} 7 \\ + 6 \\ \hline \end{array}$$

$$\begin{array}{r} 4 \\ + 9 \\ \hline \end{array}$$

$$\begin{array}{r} 9 \\ + 4 \\ \hline \end{array}$$

$$\begin{array}{r} 8 \\ + 5 \\ \hline \end{array}$$

$$\begin{array}{r} 5 \\ + 8 \\ \hline \end{array}$$

$$\begin{array}{r} 7 \\ + 6 \\ \hline \end{array} \quad \begin{array}{r} 5 \\ + 8 \\ \hline \end{array} \quad \begin{array}{r} 9 \\ + 4 \\ \hline \end{array} \quad \begin{array}{r} 6 \\ + 7 \\ \hline \end{array} \quad \begin{array}{r} 4 \\ + 9 \\ \hline \end{array} \quad \begin{array}{r} 8 \\ + 5 \\ \hline \end{array}$$

5 + 8 = _____   4 + 9 = _____   10 + 3 = _____

9 + 4 = _____   8 + 5 = _____   6 + 7 = _____

Lesson 2.5 Adding to 14

Add.

$$\begin{array}{r} 5 \\ +9 \\ \hline 14 \end{array}$$

$$\begin{array}{r} 9 \\ +5 \\ \hline \end{array}$$

$$\begin{array}{r} 8 \\ +6 \\ \hline \end{array}$$

$$\begin{array}{r} 6 \\ +8 \\ \hline \end{array}$$

$$\begin{array}{r} 7 \\ +7 \\ \hline \end{array}$$

$$\begin{array}{r} 14 \\ +0 \\ \hline \end{array}$$

$$\begin{array}{r} 9 \\ +5 \\ \hline \end{array} \qquad \begin{array}{r} 7 \\ +7 \\ \hline \end{array} \qquad \begin{array}{r} 5 \\ +9 \\ \hline \end{array} \qquad \begin{array}{r} 6 \\ +8 \\ \hline \end{array} \qquad \begin{array}{r} 0 \\ +14 \\ \hline \end{array} \qquad \begin{array}{r} 8 \\ +6 \\ \hline \end{array}$$

$10 + 4 =$ _____ $7 + 7 =$ _____ $6 + 8 =$ _____

Lesson 2.6 Adding to 15

Add.

$$\begin{array}{r} 9 \\ + 6 \\ \hline 15 \end{array}$$

$$\begin{array}{r} 6 \\ + 9 \\ \hline \end{array}$$

$$\begin{array}{r} 7 \\ + 8 \\ \hline \end{array}$$

$$\begin{array}{r} 8 \\ + 7 \\ \hline \end{array}$$

$$\begin{array}{r} 11 \\ + 4 \\ \hline \end{array}$$

$$\begin{array}{r} 4 \\ + 11 \\ \hline \end{array}$$

$$\begin{array}{r} 10 \\ + 5 \\ \hline \end{array} \qquad \begin{array}{r} 3 \\ + 12 \\ \hline \end{array} \qquad \begin{array}{r} 13 \\ + 2 \\ \hline \end{array} \qquad \begin{array}{r} 0 \\ + 15 \\ \hline \end{array} \qquad \begin{array}{r} 5 \\ + 10 \\ \hline \end{array} \qquad \begin{array}{r} 14 \\ + 1 \\ \hline \end{array}$$

$2 + 13 =$ _____ $10 + 5 =$ _____ $12 + 3 =$ _____

Lesson 2.7 Addition Facts 11–15

Add.

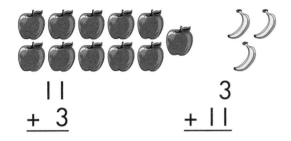 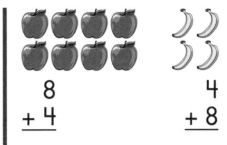

11	3
+ 3	+ 11

8	4
+ 4	+ 8

15 + 0 = _____

0 + 15 = _____

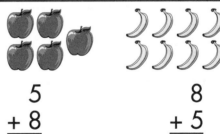

6	5
+ 5	+ 6

12	1
+ 1	+ 12

5	8
+ 8	+ 5

3 + 12 = _____

12 + 3 = _____

7
+ 7

Lesson 2.8 Problem Solving

SHOW YOUR WORK

Solve each problem.

10 are in line.

3 more line up.

How many are in line? ___13___

$$
\begin{array}{r}
10 \\
+\ 3 \\
\hline
13
\end{array}
$$

There are 7 🍁.

There are 8 🍂.

How many leaves in all? _____

There are 9 🧸 on the shelf.

There are 6 more 🧸 on the floor.

How many 🧸 in all? _____

Marcus has 5 ⚾.

Sue has 7 ⚾.

What is the sum? _____

Len has 6 ✈.

He has 6 🚚.

How many toys in all? _____

Lesson 2.8 Problem Solving

Solve each problem.

There are 6 .

There are 7 .

How many in all? ____13____

$$\begin{array}{r} 6 \\ + 7 \\ \hline 13 \end{array}$$

Rosa has 7 .

Ted ~~eats~~ ^{has} 8 .

How many in all? _____

Ivan read 9 last week.

He read 5 this week.

How many has Ivan read in all? _____

Aisha has 4 .

She has 8 .

How many in all? _____

There are 7 .

7 more come.

How many are there? _____

Lesson 2.9 Adding to 16

Add.

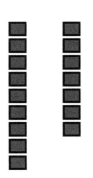

$$\begin{array}{r} 9 \\ + 7 \\ \hline 16 \end{array}$$

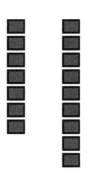

$$\begin{array}{r} 7 \\ + 9 \\ \hline \end{array}$$

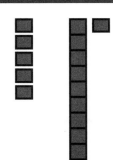

$$\begin{array}{r} 5 \\ + 11 \\ \hline \end{array}$$

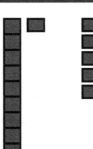

$$\begin{array}{r} 11 \\ + 5 \\ \hline \end{array}$$

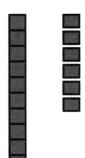

$$\begin{array}{r} 10 \\ + 6 \\ \hline \end{array}$$

$$\begin{array}{r} 6 \\ + 10 \\ \hline \end{array}$$

$$\begin{array}{r} 15 \\ + 1 \\ \hline \end{array} \qquad \begin{array}{r} 4 \\ + 12 \\ \hline \end{array} \qquad \begin{array}{r} 8 \\ + 8 \\ \hline \end{array} \qquad \begin{array}{r} 3 \\ + 13 \\ \hline \end{array} \qquad \begin{array}{r} 0 \\ + 16 \\ \hline \end{array} \qquad \begin{array}{r} 14 \\ + 2 \\ \hline \end{array}$$

$13 + 3 =$ _____ $8 + 8 =$ _____ $1 + 15 =$ _____

Lesson 2.10 Adding to 17

Add.

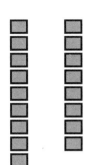

$$\begin{array}{r} 9 \\ + 8 \\ \hline 17 \end{array}$$

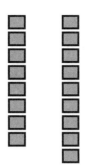

$$\begin{array}{r} 8 \\ + 9 \\ \hline \end{array}$$

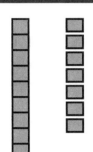

$$\begin{array}{r} 10 \\ + 7 \\ \hline \end{array}$$

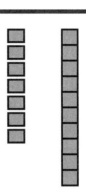

$$\begin{array}{r} 7 \\ + 10 \\ \hline \end{array}$$

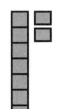 

$$\begin{array}{r} 12 \\ + 5 \\ \hline \end{array}$$

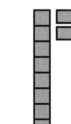

$$\begin{array}{r} 5 \\ + 12 \\ \hline \end{array}$$

$$\begin{array}{r} 2 \\ + 15 \\ \hline \end{array} \qquad \begin{array}{r} 13 \\ + 4 \\ \hline \end{array} \qquad \begin{array}{r} 16 \\ + 1 \\ \hline \end{array} \qquad \begin{array}{r} 3 \\ + 14 \\ \hline \end{array} \qquad \begin{array}{r} 11 \\ + 6 \\ \hline \end{array} \qquad \begin{array}{r} 17 \\ + 0 \\ \hline \end{array}$$

$8 + 9 =$ _____ $14 + 3 =$ _____ $6 + 11 =$ _____

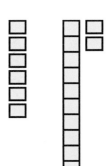

NAME _____

Lesson 2.11 Adding to 18

Add.

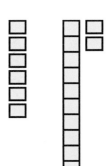
$$\begin{array}{r} 6 \\ + 12 \\ \hline 18 \end{array}$$

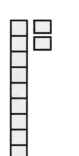
$$\begin{array}{r} 12 \\ + 6 \\ \hline \end{array}$$

$$\begin{array}{r} 10 \\ + 8 \\ \hline \end{array}$$

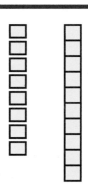
$$\begin{array}{r} 8 \\ + 10 \\ \hline \end{array}$$

$$\begin{array}{r} 13 \\ + 5 \\ \hline \end{array}$$

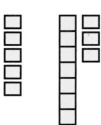
$$\begin{array}{r} 5 \\ + 13 \\ \hline \end{array}$$

$$\begin{array}{r} 9 \\ + 9 \\ \hline \end{array} \qquad \begin{array}{r} 17 \\ + 1 \\ \hline \end{array} \qquad \begin{array}{r} 7 \\ + 11 \\ \hline \end{array} \qquad \begin{array}{r} 18 \\ + 0 \\ \hline \end{array} \qquad \begin{array}{r} 2 \\ + 16 \\ \hline \end{array} \qquad \begin{array}{r} 15 \\ + 3 \\ \hline \end{array}$$

$14 + 4 =$ _____ $11 + 7 =$ _____ $9 + 9 =$ _____

Chapter 2, Lesson 11
Addition through 20

Lesson 2.12 Adding to 19

Add.

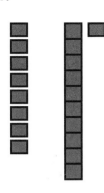
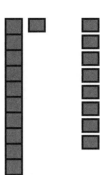

$$\begin{array}{r} 8 \\ + 11 \\ \hline 19 \end{array}$$

$$\begin{array}{r} 11 \\ + 8 \\ \hline \end{array}$$

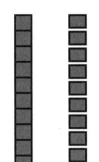
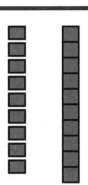

$$\begin{array}{r} 10 \\ + 9 \\ \hline \end{array}$$

$$\begin{array}{r} 9 \\ + 10 \\ \hline \end{array}$$

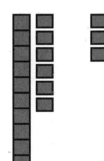

$$\begin{array}{r} 16 \\ + 3 \\ \hline \end{array}$$

$$\begin{array}{r} 3 \\ + 16 \\ \hline \end{array}$$

$$\begin{array}{r} 19 \\ + 0 \\ \hline \end{array} \qquad \begin{array}{r} 2 \\ + 17 \\ \hline \end{array} \qquad \begin{array}{r} 14 \\ + 5 \\ \hline \end{array} \qquad \begin{array}{r} 1 \\ + 18 \\ \hline \end{array} \qquad \begin{array}{r} 15 \\ + 4 \\ \hline \end{array} \qquad \begin{array}{r} 6 \\ + 13 \\ \hline \end{array}$$

$12 + 7 = $ _____ $5 + 14 = $ _____ $11 + 8 = $ _____

Lesson 2.13 Adding to 20

Add.

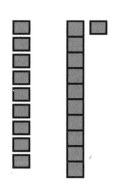

$$\begin{array}{r} 9 \\ + 11 \\ \hline 20 \end{array}$$

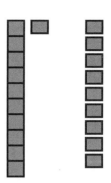

$$\begin{array}{r} 11 \\ + 9 \\ \hline \end{array}$$

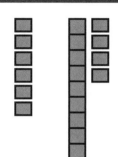

$$\begin{array}{r} 6 \\ + 14 \\ \hline \end{array}$$

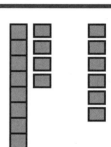

$$\begin{array}{r} 14 \\ + 6 \\ \hline \end{array}$$

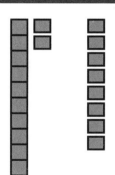

$$\begin{array}{r} 12 \\ + 8 \\ \hline \end{array}$$

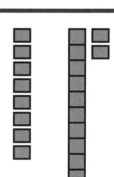

$$\begin{array}{r} 8 \\ + 12 \\ \hline \end{array}$$

$$\begin{array}{r} 10 \\ + 10 \\ \hline \end{array} \qquad \begin{array}{r} 17 \\ + 3 \\ \hline \end{array} \qquad \begin{array}{r} 4 \\ + 16 \\ \hline \end{array} \qquad \begin{array}{r} 18 \\ + 2 \\ \hline \end{array} \qquad \begin{array}{r} 5 \\ + 15 \\ \hline \end{array} \qquad \begin{array}{r} 20 \\ + 0 \\ \hline \end{array}$$

$10 + 10 =$ _____ $15 + 5 =$ _____ $1 + 19 =$ _____

Lesson 2.14 Addition Facts 16–20

Add.

14	3	5	13
+ 3	+ 14	+ 13	+ 5

2 + 16 = _____

16 + 2 = _____

14	6
+ 6	+ 14

18	1	7	10
+ 1	+ 18	+ 10	+ 7

16 + 4 = _____

4 + 16 = _____

8
+ 8

Lesson 2.15 Addition Practice through 20

Add.

7 +9	8 +3	7 +8	18 +1	8 +4	9 +8
7 +6	5 +9	8 +8	17 +3	9 +4	3 +8
2 +10	7 +5	3 +17	12 +8	15 +5	9 +9
14 +5	1 +16	3 +9	18 +2	6 +6	0 +14
16 +3	7 +7	6 +8	4 +9	12 +6	5 +15
10 +10	17 +2	11 +6	10 +0	14 +1	2 +18

Lesson 2.16 Problem Solving

Solve each problem.

There are 10 .

There are 8 🎩.

How many hats in all? ___18___

$$\begin{array}{r} 10 \\ +\ 8 \\ \hline 18 \end{array}$$

There are 7 🥄 on the table.

There are 13 🥄 in the drawer.

How many 🥄 in all? _____

Ana picked 10 🍎.

Suri picked 6 🍎.

How many 🍎 were picked? _____

There are 8 🦁.

9 more 🦁 come.

How many 🦁 are there in all? _____

Tanya has 9 🌼.

Curtis has 7 🌼.

How many 🌼 do they have in all? _____

Lesson 2.16 Problem Solving

Solve each problem.

7 ✏ broke in the morning.

9 ✏ broke in the afternoon.

How many broke? ___16___

$$\begin{array}{r} 7 \\ + 9 \\ \hline 16 \end{array}$$

There are 9 🐞.

9 more 🐞 come.

How many 🐞 are there? _____

Luisa caught 8 🐟.

She catches 9 more 🐟.

How many 🐟 did she catch in all? _____

---

10 🐰 are hopping.

6 more 🐰 begin to hop.

How many 🐰 are hopping? _____

There are 6 🔨.

There are 14 🍴.

How many tools are there in all? _____

Check What You Learned

Addition through 20

Add.

8	8	6	14	3	9
+7	+9	+7	+ 5	+8	+5

9	5	7	11	8	9
+3	+8	+9	+9	+4	+9

7	7	4	2	6	8
+5	+8	+9	+9	+9	+6

Solve each problem.

We saw 7 at the zoo.

We saw 4 at the zoo.

How many
animals did we see? _____

6  fell today.

5 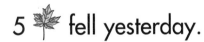 fell yesterday.

How many
leaves fell? _____

---

8 live downstairs.

6 live upstairs.

How many mice
are in the house? _____

10 are in the pond.

10 more jump in.

How many frogs
are in the pond? _____

Mid-Test Chapters 1–2

Add.

3 + 4	8 + 2	2 + 1	1 + 8	5 + 1	0 + 4
3 + 2	6 + 2	5 + 3	4 + 4	4 + 5	2 + 7
6 + 0	6 + 4	5 + 5	10 + 0	6 + 3	3 + 3

Solve each problem.

We used 4 for lunch.

We used 4 for dinner.

How many
forks were used? _____

3 🚚 are on the table.

2 🚚 are on the floor.

How many trucks
are in the room? _____

I blew up 7 🎈.

My sister blew up 2 🎈.

How many balloons
did we blow up? _____

1 🐓 crowed.

Then, 4 more 🐓 crowed.

How many
crowed in all? _____

Mid-Test Chapters 1–2

Add.

```
    7        3        7       18        8        9
  + 9      + 8      + 8      + 1      + 4      + 8
```

```
   12        5       17        5        4        9
  + 6      + 9      + 3      + 7      + 7      + 9
```

```
    6       10       12        8        5       14
  + 7      + 5      + 8      + 5      + 6      + 5
```

Solve each problem.

10 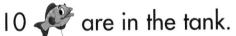 are in the tank.

4 are in the tank.

How many fish
are in the tank? _____

One bowl has 6 .

Another bowl has 5 .

What is
the sum? _____

The candy shop sold
12 on Monday.

The shop sold 8 on Tuesday.

How many have
sold so far this week? _____

7 stood on the cliff.

8 stood under the cliff.

How many
goats in all? _____

Spectrum Addition
Grade 1

NAME _____

 Check What You Know

Addition Equations and Strategies

Write a number to complete each equation.

$16 + 2 = \boxed{}$ | $\boxed{} + 3 = 11$ | $7 + 3 = \boxed{} + 7$

$8 + 2 = 5 + \boxed{}$ | $9 + 5 = 5 + \boxed{}$ | $11 + 3 = \boxed{} + 7$

$20 = \boxed{}$ | $6 + \boxed{} = 8 + 7$ | $4 + 6 = 10 + \boxed{}$

Write any numbers in the blanks to make the equations correct.

$8 + 4 = \boxed{} + \boxed{}$ $\boxed{} + \boxed{} = 2 + 3$

Circle equations that are true. Draw an X on equations that are not true.

$$\begin{array}{r} 18 \\ + 1 \\ \hline 20 \end{array} \qquad \begin{array}{r} 8 \\ + 7 \\ \hline 18 \end{array} \qquad \begin{array}{r} 14 \\ + 6 \\ \hline 20 \end{array} \qquad \begin{array}{r} 3 \\ + 8 \\ \hline 11 \end{array}$$

Check What You Know

Addition Equations and Strategies

Add by counting on.

How many is 4 more than 8 🐞? _____

What is 6 more than 4 🍁? _____

Think about how to make each equation easier to solve. Write a number in the blank.

$7 + 5 =$ $2 + 5 + 5 =$ $2 + \boxed{} = 12$

$6 + 7 =$ $6 + 6 + 1 =$ $12 + \boxed{} = 13$

Add.

$$\begin{array}{r} 8 \\ 2 \\ + 4 \\ \hline \end{array} \qquad \begin{array}{r} 9 \\ 5 \\ + 5 \\ \hline \end{array} \qquad \begin{array}{r} 12 \\ 3 \\ + 2 \\ \hline \end{array} \qquad \begin{array}{r} 3 \\ 8 \\ + 1 \\ \hline \end{array}$$

Lesson 3.1 Addition Equations

In an equation, the numbers before the equal sign (=) are equal to the numbers after the equal sign.

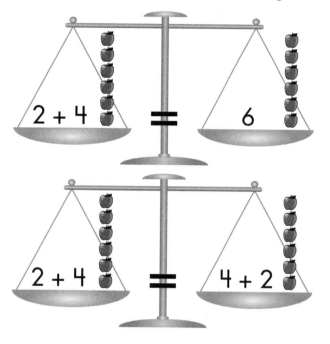

$$
\begin{array}{r}
2 \\
+\ 4 \\
\hline
6
\end{array}
\Big\}
$$

An equation like this uses a line instead of an equal sign. The line means "equal to."

Write a number to complete each equation.

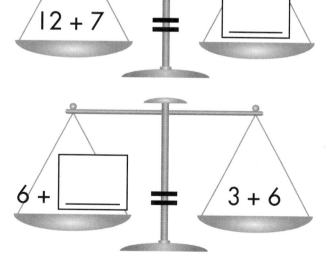

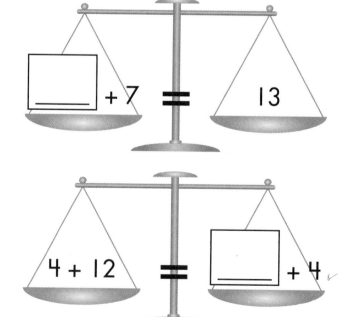

Lesson 3.1 Addition Equations

Write a number to complete each equation.

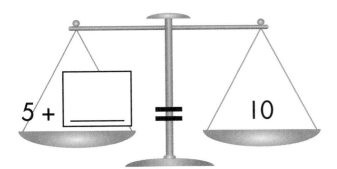

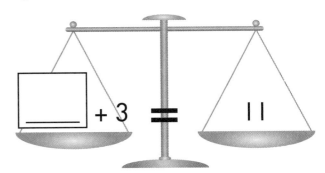

$5 + \boxed{} = 10$

$\boxed{} + 3 = 11$

$4 + 3 = \boxed{}$	$2 + 6 = 6 + \boxed{}$	$\boxed{} + 12 = 12 + 3$
$8 + \boxed{} = 16$	$4 + 3 = \boxed{} + 4$	$0 + 4 = 4 + \boxed{}$
$\boxed{} + 1 = 20$	$10 + \boxed{} = 1 + 10$	$9 + \boxed{} = 5 + 9$
$13 + \boxed{} = 19$	$\boxed{} + 7 = 7 + 8$	$5 + 10 = 10 + \boxed{}$

NAME _____

Lesson 3.2 Completing Equations

The numbers before and after the equal sign may look the same or different. As long as they are equal, the equation is correct.

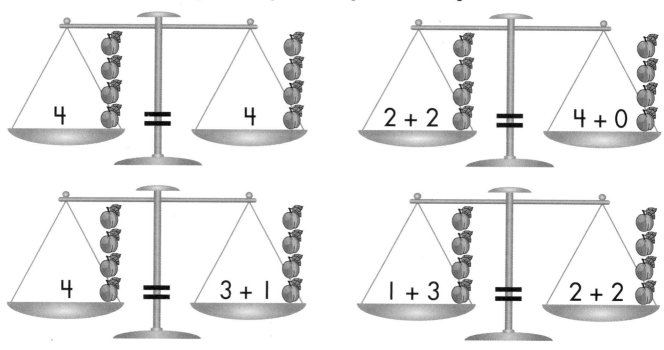

Write a number to complete each equation.

$8 = \boxed{}$ $10 = 4 + \boxed{}$ $0 + 5 = 5 + \boxed{}$

$5 + 2 = \boxed{} + 5$ $6 + 2 = 4 + \boxed{}$ $14 + 4 = 9 + \boxed{}$

$15 + 5 = \boxed{}$ $4 + 9 = \boxed{} + 3$ $3 + \boxed{} = 3 + 1 + 1$

Lesson 3.2 Completing Equations

Write any numbers in the blanks to make each equation correct.

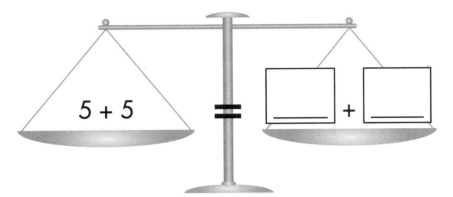

$$5 + 5 = \boxed{} + \boxed{}$$

$\boxed{} + \boxed{} = 6 + 2$

$0 + 8 = \boxed{} + \boxed{}$

$9 + 5 = \boxed{} + \boxed{}$

$\boxed{} + \boxed{} = 6 + 3$

$\boxed{} + \boxed{} = 7 + 3$

$14 + 2 = \boxed{} + \boxed{}$

$17 + 3 = \boxed{} + \boxed{}$

$\boxed{} + \boxed{} = 4 + 3$

$\boxed{} + \boxed{} = 11 + 4$

$3 + 3 = \boxed{} + \boxed{}$

Lesson 3.3 Completing Equation Pairs

Write the same number to complete each pair of equations.

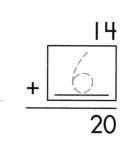

$$14 + \boxed{6} \over 20 \qquad \boxed{6} + 4 \over 10 \qquad 5 + \boxed{} \over 13 \qquad \boxed{} + 12 \over 20$$

$$\boxed{} + 3 \over 18 \qquad 10 + 5 \over \boxed{} \qquad 16 + \boxed{} \over 16 \qquad \boxed{} + 3 \over 3$$

$$9 + \boxed{} \over 11 \qquad 0 + \boxed{} \over 2 \qquad 16 + 3 \over \boxed{} \qquad \boxed{} + 1 \over 20$$

$$\boxed{} + 3 \over 15 \qquad 8 + 4 \over \boxed{} \qquad \boxed{} + 7 \over 14 \qquad 8 + \boxed{} \over 15$$

Lesson 3.4 Evaluating Equations

If the numbers before the equal sign (=) do not equal the numbers after the equal sign, the equation is not true.

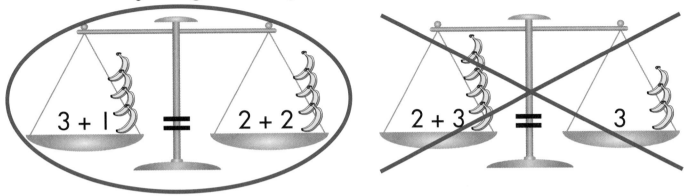

Circle each equation that is true. Draw an X through each equation that is not true.

$10 + 7 = 17$	$8 + 6 = 16$	$12 + 3 = 12 + 2 + 2$
$8 + 2 = 5 + 5$	$5 + 9 = 9 + 5$	$4 + 7 = 12$
$\begin{array}{r} 10 \\ + 7 \\ \hline 11 \end{array}$	$\begin{array}{r} 8 \\ + 6 \\ \hline 14 \end{array}$	$\begin{array}{r} 9 \\ + 9 \\ \hline 18 \end{array}$
$\begin{array}{r} 0 \\ + 10 \\ \hline 11 \end{array}$	$\begin{array}{r} 5 \\ + 3 \\ \hline 8 \end{array}$	$\begin{array}{r} 17 \\ + 2 \\ \hline 20 \end{array}$

Lesson 3.5 Counting On

One way to add to a number is to count ahead.

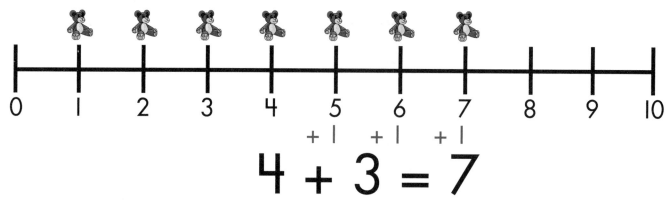

$$4 + 3 = 7$$

Add by counting on.

How many is 2 more than 7 🐱? ____9____   7 + 2 = 9

What is 1 more than 8 🐶? _____

How many is 1 more than 9 🦋? _____

What is 3 more than 16 🐐? _____

There are 4 more than 13 🐕. How many 🐕 are there? _____

How many is 5 more than 12 🌼? _____

Lesson 3.6 Doubles and Near-Doubles

Add to find the sum.

$$\begin{array}{r} 2 \\ +\ 2 \\ \hline 4 \end{array}$$

$$3 + 3 = \underline{\quad 6 \quad} + 1 = \underline{\quad 7 \quad}$$

$$1 + 1 = \underline{\qquad} + 1 = \underline{\qquad}$$

$$\begin{array}{r} 5 \\ +\ 5 \\ \hline \end{array}$$

$$\begin{array}{r} 3 \\ +\ 3 \\ \hline \end{array}$$

$$4 + 4 = \underline{\qquad} + 1 = \underline{\qquad}$$

$$\begin{array}{r} 4 \\ +\ 4 \\ \hline \end{array}$$

$$\begin{array}{r} 1 \\ +\ 1 \\ \hline \end{array}$$

$$2 + 2 = \underline{\qquad} + 1 = \underline{\qquad}$$

$$3 + 3 = \underline{\qquad} + 1 = \underline{\qquad}$$

Lesson 3.7 Making 10

One way to add is to think about what equals 10.

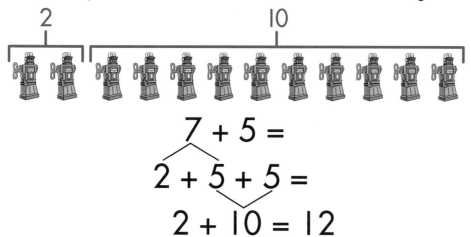

$$7 + 5 =$$
$$2 + 5 + 5 =$$
$$2 + 10 = 12$$

Write a number in each blank. Think about what equals 10.

$$8 + 6 = \qquad 8 + 2 + 4 = \qquad 10 + \boxed{} = 14$$

$$7 + 6 = \qquad 7 + 3 + 3 = \qquad 10 + \boxed{} = 13$$

Lesson 3.8 Making Known Sums

One way to add is to think about equations (like doubles) that are easy to solve.

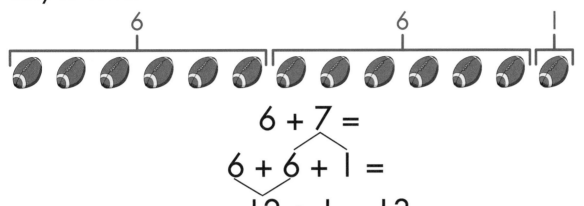

$$6 + 7 =$$
$$6 + 6 + 1 =$$
$$12 + 1 = 13$$

Write a number in each blank. Think about what equals 10.

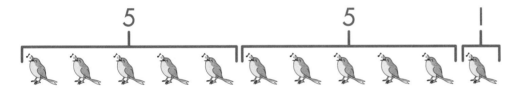

$5 + 6 =$ $5 + 5 + 1 =$ $10 + \boxed{} = 11$

$7 + 8 =$ $7 + 7 + 1 =$ $14 + \boxed{} = 15$

Lesson 3.9 Adding 3 Numbers

	Add the ones.	Add the tens.

```
                                        ↓              ↓
12  ☐☐☐☐☐☐☐☐☐ ☐☐     12             12
 4        ☐☐☐☐          4              4
+3         ☐☐☐        + 3            + 3
                       ───    sum = ─────
                        9            19
```

Add.

```
  10        11         4        15         2
   5         3         3         3         2
+  3       + 5       + 2       + 2       + 2


   2         8        12         2         1
   4         2         4         3         1
+  1       + 1       + 1       + 3       + 4


   5        15        13        11        12
   4         1         2         6         2
+  1       + 1       + 1       + 2       + 6
```

Lesson 3.10 Making 10 to Add 3 Numbers

When you add three numbers, look for two numbers that equal ten. Rewrite to make the equation easier to solve.

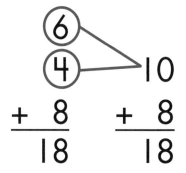

Look at each pair of equations. In the first equation, circle two numbers that equal 10. Write the missing number in the second equation.

$$
\begin{array}{r} 5 \\ 5 \\ +\ 7 \\ \hline 17 \end{array}
\qquad
\begin{array}{r} 10 \\ +\ \boxed{} \\ \hline 17 \end{array}
\qquad\bigg|\qquad
\begin{array}{r} 4 \\ 6 \\ +\ 9 \\ \hline 19 \end{array}
\qquad
\begin{array}{r} 10 \\ +\ \boxed{} \\ \hline 19 \end{array}
$$

$$
\begin{array}{r} 6 \\ 2 \\ +\ 8 \\ \hline 16 \end{array}
\qquad
\begin{array}{r} 6 \\ +\ \boxed{} \\ \hline 16 \end{array}
\qquad\bigg|\qquad
\begin{array}{r} 5 \\ 8 \\ +\ 2 \\ \hline 15 \end{array}
\qquad
\begin{array}{r} \boxed{} \\ +\ 10 \\ \hline 15 \end{array}
$$

$$
\begin{array}{r} 9 \\ 1 \\ +\ 2 \\ \hline 12 \end{array}
\qquad
\begin{array}{r} 10 \\ +\ \boxed{} \\ \hline 12 \end{array}
\qquad\bigg|\qquad
\begin{array}{r} 6 \\ 9 \\ +\ 1 \\ \hline 16 \end{array}
\qquad
\begin{array}{r} 6 \\ +\ \boxed{} \\ \hline 16 \end{array}
$$

NAME _____

Lesson 3.11 Problem Solving

Solve each problem.

Lanie has 10 🦕.

Tina has 2 🦖. Paul has 5 🦖.

How many 🦖 do they have in all? ___17___

$$\begin{array}{r} 10 \\ 2 \\ + 5 \\ \hline 17 \end{array}$$

The toy store sold 7 🤖 in March,

3 🤖 in April, and 8 🤖 in May.

How many 🤖 did the toy store sell in all? _____

Felicia puts 2 🪆, 2 🧸, and

8 🐭 on shelves. How many

toys does Felicia put on shelves? _____

The toy store has 8 🚗, 2 🚚,

and 10 🚜. How many of these

toys does the toy store have in all? _____

The bakery sells 4 🧁 on Monday, 10 🧁

on Tuesday, and 6 🧁 on Wednesday.

How many 🧁 did the bakery sell? _____

Check What You Learned

Addition Equations and Strategies

Write a number to complete each equation.

$11 + 3 = \boxed{}$ | $9 + 1 = \boxed{} + 9$ | $7 + 5 = 6 + \boxed{}$

$14 + 4 = \boxed{} + 7$ | $9 + \boxed{} = 5 + 11$ | $12 + 3 = 8 + \boxed{}$

Write any numbers in the blanks to make the equations correct.

$12 + 3 = \boxed{} + \boxed{}$ $\boxed{} + \boxed{} = 0 + 8$

Write the same number to complete each pair of equations.

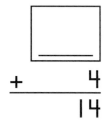
$$\begin{array}{r} \boxed{} \\ + \quad 4 \\ \hline 14 \end{array}$$

$$\begin{array}{r} 2 \\ + \boxed{} \\ \hline 12 \end{array}$$

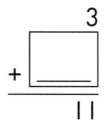
$$\begin{array}{r} 3 \\ + \boxed{} \\ \hline 11 \end{array}$$

$$\begin{array}{r} 4 \\ + \quad 4 \\ \hline \boxed{} \end{array}$$

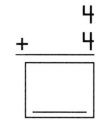

Circle equations that are true. Draw an X on equations that are not true.

$$\begin{array}{r} 6 \\ + 12 \\ \hline 18 \end{array} \qquad \begin{array}{r} 10 \\ 3 \\ + \ 6 \\ \hline 20 \end{array} \qquad \begin{array}{r} 9 \\ + 7 \\ \hline 17 \end{array} \qquad \begin{array}{r} 4 \\ 3 \\ + 1 \\ \hline 8 \end{array}$$

Check What You Learned

Addition Equations and Strategies

Add by counting on.

How many is 6 more than 5 ? _____

Think about how to make each equation easier to solve. Write a number in the blank.

$8 + 3 =$ $8 + 2 + 1 =$ $10 + \boxed{} = 11$

$7 + 8 =$ $7 + 7 + 1 =$ $\boxed{} + 1 = 15$

Add.

$$\begin{array}{r} 5 \\ 5 \\ +8 \\ \hline \end{array} \qquad \begin{array}{r} 11 \\ 6 \\ +2 \\ \hline \end{array} \qquad \begin{array}{r} 2 \\ 9 \\ +4 \\ \hline \end{array} \qquad \begin{array}{r} 1 \\ 7 \\ +3 \\ \hline \end{array}$$

On the table, there are 10 🍴, 3 🥤, and 5 🍽. How many things are on the table? _____

Check What You Know

Addition through 100

Add.

37 + 2	43 + 5	81 + 4	23 + 1	56 + 2
44 + 6	77 + 3	69 + 2	19 + 3	46 + 4
14 + 10	39 + 20	42 + 30	21 + 40	18 + 30
55 + 40	82 + 10	62 + 30	11 + 80	22 + 60

Write a number to answer each question.

What is 10 more than 16? _____

What is 10 more than 65? _____

What is 10 more than 78? _____

What is 10 more than 46? _____

Lesson 4.1 Adding 2-Digit and 1-Digit Numbers

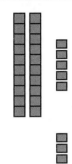

	First add ones.	Then, add tens.
25 + 3	25 + 3 8	25 + 3 sum = 28

Add the ones.	Put the ones in the ones place. Put the ten in the tens place.	Add the tens.
38 8 + 4 + 4 ? 12 12 = 1 ten and 2 ones	1 38 + 4 2	1 38 + 4 sum = 42

Add.

15 + 2	19 + 6	27 + 5	20 + 6	13 + 4

38 + 8	22 + 6	29 + 3	47 + 2	14 + 1

63 + 5	53 + 6	87 + 2	41 + 4	79 + 9

Lesson 4.1 Adding 2-Digit and 1-Digit Numbers

Add.

63 + 6	42 + 5	29 + 9	71 + 8	62 + 3
45 + 4	19 + 6	30 + 9	16 + 7	22 + 4
30 + 6	81 + 7	47 + 2	56 + 5	48 + 7
15 + 8	67 + 1	42 + 3	56 + 4	39 + 5
23 + 8	17 + 7	44 + 6	16 + 3	86 + 6
90 + 4	31 + 9	68 + 4	24 + 5	36 + 8

NAME _____

Lesson 4.2 Adding Multiples of 10 to 2-Digit Numbers

6 tens and 8 ones plus 2 tens equals 8 tens and 8 ones.

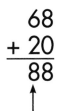
```
  68
+ 20
----
  88
```
↑

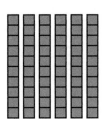   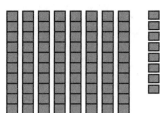

Only the tens
place changes.

Use the pictures to help you add.

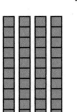 +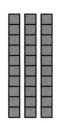
```
  42
+ 30
```

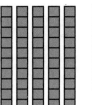 +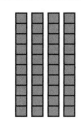
```
  58
+ 40
```

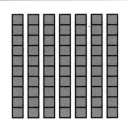 +
```
  74
+ 10
```

NAME _____

Lesson 4.2 Adding Multiples of 10 to 2-Digit Numbers

Add.

15 + 10	19 + 20	23 + 20	31 + 10	47 + 20
13 + 30	29 + 40	17 + 40	11 + 50	60 + 30
75 + 10	50 + 40	25 + 70	42 + 50	12 + 80
18 + 20	12 + 80	20 + 40	59 + 20	15 + 70
17 + 40	11 + 20	49 + 30	86 + 10	25 + 70
25 + 30	63 + 20	18 + 50	46 + 40	72 + 20

Lesson 4.3 Adding 10 Mentally

Add 10 to each number. Solve the problem only in your mind.
Write the number in the thought bubble.

38

64

13

56

87

54

11

90

26

8

2

43

Lesson 4.4 Problem Solving

SHOW YOUR WORK

Solve each problem.

There are 23 🐛.

10 more 🐛 are blown up.

How many 🐛 are there now? _____ 33

```
  23
+ 10
-----
  33
```

There are 15 🍑 in a basket.

There are 9 🍑 in a bowl.

How many 🍑 in all? _____

There are 31 🦢 in the pond.

7 🦢 are on the grass.

How many 🦢 in all? _____

There are 27 ✏ on the table.

There are 6 ✏ in the box.

How many ✏ in all? _____

There are 56 🍁 on the ground.

20 🍁 fall from the tree.

How many 🍁 are on the ground now? _____

There are 34 🐕 in the dog park.

30 more 🐕 come.

What is 34 plus 30? _____

Lesson 4.4 Problem Solving

Solve each problem.

There are 30 🐦 on the roof.

10 more 🐦 land on the roof.

How many are on the roof? _____

I have 19 🍌.

I have 6 🪙.

What is the sum? _____

There are 40 🧃.

There are 40 🥤.

How many in all? _____

There are 38 🚓.

8 more 🚓 drive up.

How many 🚓 are there in all? _____

Mr. Lin has 26 ✏️.

Ms. Brown has 50 ✏️.

How many ✏️ in all? _____

Lesson 4.5 Addition Practice through 100

Add.

9 + 8	9 + 7	16 + 9	27 + 8	28 + 5	37 + 7
49 + 9	67 + 9	58 + 7	18 + 9	78 + 6	96 + 4
87 + 6	29 + 5	79 + 6	8 + 8	46 + 8	66 + 7
36 + 10	15 + 10	78 + 10	89 + 10	9 + 10	47 + 10
22 + 40	63 + 30	35 + 50	71 + 20	27 + 30	43 + 40
59 + 20	80 + 10	16 + 40	12 + 70	13 + 60	17 + 80

Check What You Learned

Addition through 100

Add.

12 + 4	18 + 2	15 + 3	17 + 1	13 + 6
35 + 7	48 + 1	56 + 6	79 + 2	22 + 6
83 + 10	14 + 10	36 + 10	41 + 10	90 + 10
54 + 10	10 + 10	17 + 10	25 + 10	67 + 10
27 + 20	33 + 30	48 + 30	62 + 20	19 + 40
50 + 20	62 + 10	49 + 20	38 + 40	11 + 60

Final Test Chapters 1–4

Add.

5	3	8	4	0	2
+ 4	+ 2	+ 1	+ 4	+ 9	+ 8

6	7	9	2	1	0
+ 3	+ 0	+ 1	+ 3	+ 5	+ 4

4	2	6	1	0	4
+ 6	+ 7	+ 0	+ 6	+ 8	+ 1

1	3	5	8	5	6
+ 0	+ 3	+ 2	+ 2	+ 3	+ 1

Solve each problem.

7	3
+ 3	+ 7

5	2
+ 2	+ 5

Imala has 5 .

She has 3 ⬤══════.

What is 5 plus 3? _____

There are 6 .

4 more 🦛 come.

What is 6 + 4? _____

Final Test Chapters 1–4

Add.

8	9	7	8	8	15
+ 4	+ 2	+ 8	+ 9	+ 8	+ 5

6	7	9	7	6	12
+ 8	+ 5	+ 9	+ 7	+ 7	+ 7

9	6	9	10	6	8
+ 8	+ 9	+ 7	+ 9	+ 6	+ 5

16	14	11	19	10	13
+ 2	+ 3	+ 3	+ 0	+ 3	+ 3

Solve each problem.

Pamela bought 10 .

She bought 8 .

How many did she buy? _____

There are 7 .

9 more fly in.

How many in all? _____

Myron counted 12 .

He counted 3 more .

How many did he count? _____

There are 7 in the tree.

6 more run up the tree.

How many are in the tree? _____

Final Test Chapters 1–4

Write a number to complete each equation.

$12 + 7 = \boxed{} + 12$ | $\boxed{} + 2 = 7$ | $15 + 5 = 7 + \boxed{}$

$10 = 2 + 2 + \boxed{}$ | $4 + 4 = 1 + \boxed{}$ | $\boxed{} + 11 = 7 + 6$

Write the same number to complete each pair of equations.

$$\begin{array}{r} \boxed{} \\ + \quad 9 \\ \hline 15 \end{array} \qquad \begin{array}{r} 3 \\ + \quad 3 \\ \hline \boxed{} \end{array} \qquad \Big| \qquad \begin{array}{r} 12 \\ + \quad 2 \\ \hline \boxed{} \end{array} \qquad \begin{array}{r} 4 \\ + \boxed{} \\ \hline 18 \end{array}$$

Circle equations that are true. Draw an X on equations that are not true.

$$\begin{array}{r} 8 \\ + 12 \\ \hline 20 \end{array} \qquad \begin{array}{r} 4 \\ + 11 \\ \hline 15 \end{array} \qquad \begin{array}{r} 9 \\ + 7 \\ \hline 16 \end{array} \qquad \begin{array}{r} 5 \\ + 5 \\ \hline 50 \end{array}$$

Answer each question.

What is 2 more than 17? _____

What is 6 more than 8? _____

Final Test Chapters 1-4

Write a number in each blank to make the equation true.

6 + 5 =

1 + 5 + 5 =

1 + ☐ = 11

6 + 8 =

6 + 6 + 2 =

12 + ☐ = 14

Add.

$$\begin{array}{r} 12 \\ 3 \\ +\ 2 \\ \hline \end{array} \qquad \begin{array}{r} 10 \\ 5 \\ +\ 5 \\ \hline \end{array} \qquad \begin{array}{r} 14 \\ 2 \\ +\ 3 \\ \hline \end{array} \qquad \begin{array}{r} 8 \\ 9 \\ +1 \\ \hline \end{array} \qquad \begin{array}{r} 4 \\ 7 \\ +6 \\ \hline \end{array}$$

$$\begin{array}{r} 11 \\ 4 \\ +\ 1 \\ \hline \end{array} \qquad \begin{array}{r} 9 \\ 6 \\ +\ 5 \\ \hline \end{array} \qquad \begin{array}{r} 13 \\ 1 \\ +\ 2 \\ \hline \end{array} \qquad \begin{array}{r} 7 \\ 8 \\ +2 \\ \hline \end{array} \qquad \begin{array}{r} 3 \\ 6 \\ +5 \\ \hline \end{array}$$

Add.

$$\begin{array}{r} 15 \\ +4 \\ \hline \end{array} \qquad \begin{array}{r} 19 \\ +3 \\ \hline \end{array} \qquad \begin{array}{r} 54 \\ +7 \\ \hline \end{array} \qquad \begin{array}{r} 28 \\ +4 \\ \hline \end{array} \qquad \begin{array}{r} 13 \\ +5 \\ \hline \end{array} \qquad \begin{array}{r} 75 \\ +6 \\ \hline \end{array}$$

$$\begin{array}{r} 58 \\ +10 \\ \hline \end{array} \qquad \begin{array}{r} 43 \\ +10 \\ \hline \end{array} \qquad \begin{array}{r} 87 \\ +10 \\ \hline \end{array} \qquad \begin{array}{r} 11 \\ +10 \\ \hline \end{array} \qquad \begin{array}{r} 41 \\ +10 \\ \hline \end{array} \qquad \begin{array}{r} 26 \\ +10 \\ \hline \end{array}$$

Scoring Record for Posttests, Mid-Test, and Final Test

Chapter Posttest	Your Score	Performance			
		Excellent	Very Good	Fair	Needs Improvement
1	___ of 44	44	40–43	31–39	30 or fewer
2	___ of 22	22	20–21	15–19	14 or fewer
3	___ of 24	24	21–23	17–20	16 or fewer
4	___ of 30	30	27–29	21–26	20 or fewer
Mid-Test	___ of 22	22	20–21	15–19	14 or fewer
Final Test	___ of 98	98	88–97	69–87	68 or fewer

Record your test score in the Your Score column. See where your score falls in the Performance columns. If your score is fair or needs improvement, review the chapter material again.

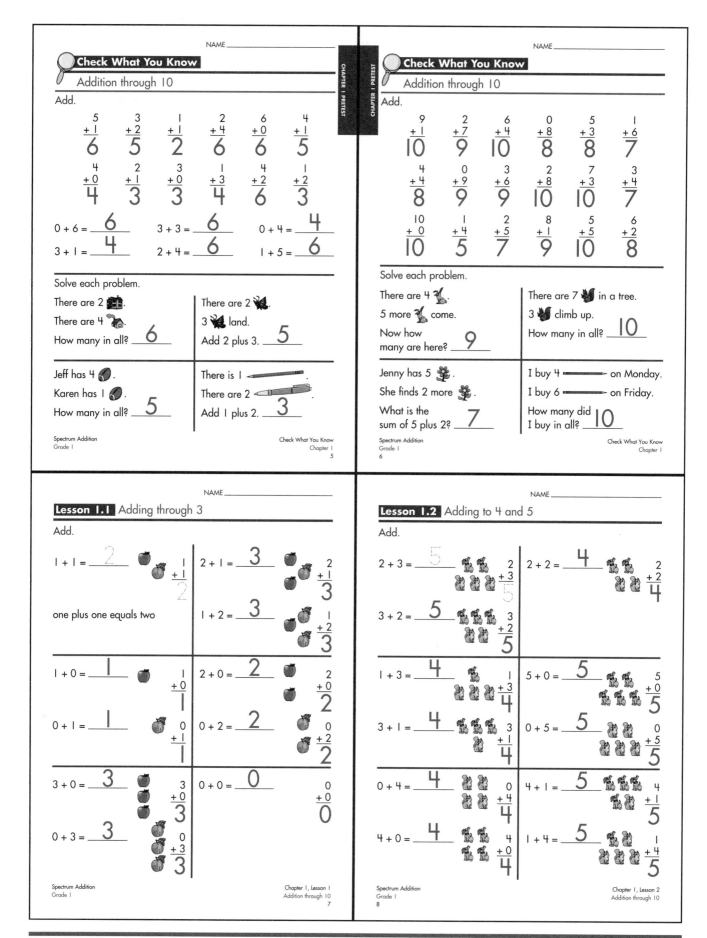

Check What You Know
Addition through 10

Add.

5 +1 = **6**	3 +2 = **5**	1 +1 = **2**	2 +4 = **6**	6 +0 = **6**	4 +1 = **5**
4 +0 = **4**	2 +1 = **3**	3 +0 = **3**	1 +3 = **4**	4 +2 = **6**	1 +2 = **3**

0 + 6 = **6**   3 + 3 = **6**   0 + 4 = **4**

3 + 1 = **4**   2 + 4 = **6**   1 + 5 = **6**

Solve each problem.

There are 2 🏫.
There are 4 🏠.
How many in all? **6**

There are 2 🦋.
3 🦋 land.
Add 2 plus 3. **5**

Jeff has 4 🏈.
Karen has 1 🏈.
How many in all? **5**

There is 1 ✏️.
There are 2 🖊️.
Add 1 plus 2. **3**

Check What You Know
Addition through 10

Add.

9 +1 = **10**	2 +7 = **9**	6 +4 = **10**	0 +8 = **8**	5 +3 = **8**	1 +6 = **7**
4 +4 = **8**	0 +9 = **9**	3 +6 = **9**	2 +8 = **10**	7 +3 = **10**	3 +4 = **7**
10 +0 = **10**	1 +4 = **5**	2 +5 = **7**	8 +1 = **9**	5 +5 = **10**	6 +2 = **8**

Solve each problem.

There are 4 🐰.
5 more 🐰 come.
Now how
many are here? **9**

There are 7 🐿️ in a tree.
3 🐿️ climb up.
How many in all? **10**

Jenny has 5 🌳.
She finds 2 more 🌳.
What is the
sum of 5 plus 2? **7**

I buy 4 ✏️ on Monday.
I buy 6 ✏️ on Friday.
How many did
I buy in all? **10**

Lesson 1.1 Adding through 3

Add.

1 + 1 = **2**   🍎 1 +1 = **2**

one plus one equals two

2 + 1 = **3**   🍎🍎 2 +1 = **3**

1 + 2 = **3**   🍎 1 +2 = **3**

1 + 0 = **1**   🍎 1 +0 = **1**

2 + 0 = **2**   🍎🍎 2 +0 = **2**

0 + 1 = **1**   🍎 0 +1 = **1**

0 + 2 = **2**   🍎 0 +2 = **2**

3 + 0 = **3**   🍎🍎🍎 3 +0 = **3**

0 + 0 = **0**   0 +0 = **0**

0 + 3 = **3**   🍎🍎🍎 0 +3 = **3**

Lesson 1.2 Adding to 4 and 5

Add.

2 + 3 = **5**   🐿️🐿️🐿️🐿️🐿️ 2 +3 = **5**

3 + 2 = **5**   🐿️🐿️🐿️🐿️🐿️ 3 +2 = **5**

2 + 2 = **4**   🐿️🐿️🐿️🐿️ 2 +2 = **4**

1 + 3 = **4**   🐿️🐿️🐿️🐿️ 1 +3 = **4**

3 + 1 = **4**   🐿️🐿️🐿️🐿️ 3 +1 = **4**

5 + 0 = **5**   🐿️🐿️🐿️🐿️🐿️ 5 +0 = **5**

0 + 5 = **5**   🐿️🐿️🐿️🐿️🐿️ 0 +5 = **5**

0 + 4 = **4**   🐿️🐿️🐿️🐿️ 0 +4 = **4**

4 + 1 = **5**   🐿️🐿️🐿️🐿️🐿️ 4 +1 = **5**

4 + 0 = **4**   🐿️🐿️🐿️🐿️ 4 +0 = **4**

1 + 4 = **5**   🐿️🐿️🐿️🐿️🐿️ 1 +4 = **5**

Lesson 1.3 Adding to 6

Add.

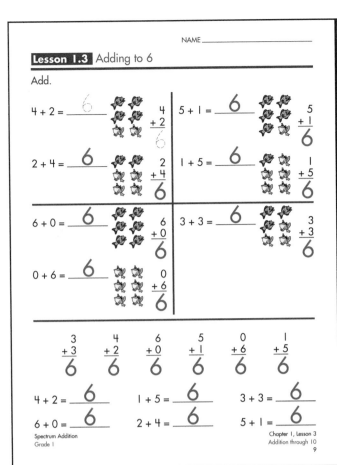

$4 + 2 =$ _6_ $\begin{array}{r} 4 \\ +2 \\ \hline 6 \end{array}$ $5 + 1 =$ _6_ $\begin{array}{r} 5 \\ +1 \\ \hline 6 \end{array}$

$2 + 4 =$ _6_ $\begin{array}{r} 2 \\ +4 \\ \hline 6 \end{array}$ $1 + 5 =$ _6_ $\begin{array}{r} 1 \\ +5 \\ \hline 6 \end{array}$

$6 + 0 =$ _6_ $\begin{array}{r} 6 \\ +0 \\ \hline 6 \end{array}$ $3 + 3 =$ _6_ $\begin{array}{r} 3 \\ +3 \\ \hline 6 \end{array}$

$0 + 6 =$ _6_ $\begin{array}{r} 0 \\ +6 \\ \hline 6 \end{array}$

$\begin{array}{r} 3 \\ +3 \\ \hline 6 \end{array}$ $\begin{array}{r} 4 \\ +2 \\ \hline 6 \end{array}$ $\begin{array}{r} 6 \\ +0 \\ \hline 6 \end{array}$ $\begin{array}{r} 5 \\ +1 \\ \hline 6 \end{array}$ $\begin{array}{r} 0 \\ +6 \\ \hline 6 \end{array}$ $\begin{array}{r} 1 \\ +5 \\ \hline 6 \end{array}$

$4 + 2 =$ _6_ $1 + 5 =$ _6_ $3 + 3 =$ _6_

$6 + 0 =$ _6_ $2 + 4 =$ _6_ $5 + 1 =$ _6_

Lesson 1.4 Addition Facts 0–6

Add.

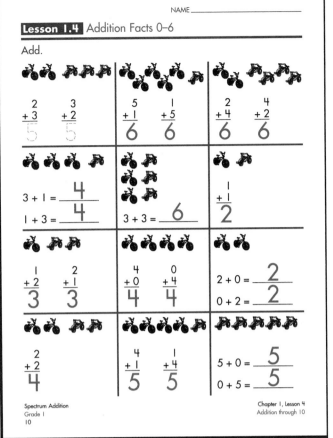

$\begin{array}{r} 2 \\ +3 \\ \hline 5 \end{array}$ $\begin{array}{r} 3 \\ +2 \\ \hline 5 \end{array}$ $\begin{array}{r} 5 \\ +1 \\ \hline 6 \end{array}$ $\begin{array}{r} 1 \\ +5 \\ \hline 6 \end{array}$ $\begin{array}{r} 2 \\ +4 \\ \hline 6 \end{array}$ $\begin{array}{r} 4 \\ +2 \\ \hline 6 \end{array}$

$3 + 1 =$ _4_
$1 + 3 =$ _4_ $3 + 3 =$ _6_ $\begin{array}{r} 1 \\ +1 \\ \hline 2 \end{array}$

$\begin{array}{r} 1 \\ +2 \\ \hline 3 \end{array}$ $\begin{array}{r} 2 \\ +1 \\ \hline 3 \end{array}$ $\begin{array}{r} 4 \\ +0 \\ \hline 4 \end{array}$ $\begin{array}{r} 0 \\ +4 \\ \hline 4 \end{array}$ $2 + 0 =$ _2_
$0 + 2 =$ _2_

$\begin{array}{r} 2 \\ +2 \\ \hline 4 \end{array}$ $\begin{array}{r} 4 \\ +1 \\ \hline 5 \end{array}$ $\begin{array}{r} 1 \\ +4 \\ \hline 5 \end{array}$ $5 + 0 =$ _5_
$0 + 5 =$ _5_

Lesson 1.5 Problem Solving   **SHOW YOUR WORK**

Solve each problem.

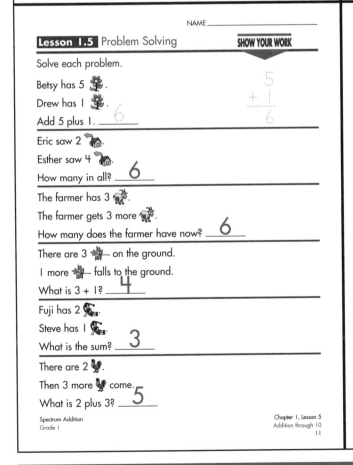

Betsy has 5 🐝.
Drew has 1 🌸.
Add 5 plus 1. _6_ $\begin{array}{r} 5 \\ +1 \\ \hline 6 \end{array}$

Eric saw 2 🏠.
Esther saw 4 🏠.
How many in all? _6_

The farmer has 3 🐐.
The farmer gets 3 more 🐐.
How many does the farmer have now? _6_

There are 3 🍁 on the ground.
1 more 🍁 falls to the ground.
What is 3 + 1? _4_

Fuji has 2 🐱.
Steve has 1 🐱.
What is the sum? _3_

There are 2 🐓.
Then 3 more 🐓 come.
What is 2 plus 3? _5_

Lesson 1.5 Problem Solving   **SHOW YOUR WORK**

Solve each problem.

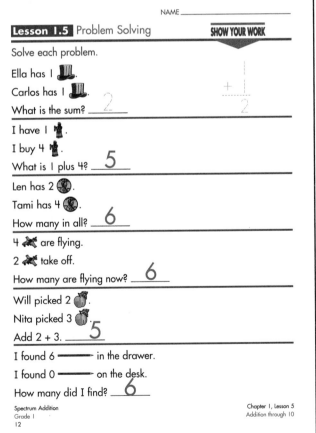

Ella has 1 🎩.
Carlos has 1 🎩.
What is the sum? _2_ $\begin{array}{r} 1 \\ +1 \\ \hline 2 \end{array}$

I have 1 🌽.
I buy 4 🌽.
What is 1 plus 4? _5_

Len has 2 🌐.
Tami has 4 🌐.
How many in all? _6_

4 ✈ are flying.
2 ✈ take off.
How many are flying now? _6_

Will picked 2 🎃.
Nita picked 3 🎃.
Add 2 + 3. _5_

I found 6 _____ in the drawer.
I found 0 _____ on the desk.
How many did I find? _6_

Spectrum Addition
Grade 1

Answer Key

Lesson 1.6 Adding to 7

Add.

5 + 2 = 7   5 +2 7

3 + 4 = 7   3 +4 7

2 + 5 = 7   2 +5 7

4 + 3 = 7   4 +3 7

6 + 1 = 7   6 +1 7

7 + 0 = 7   7 +0 7

1 + 6 = 7   1 +6 7

0 + 7 = 7   0 +7 7

3 +4 7   2 +5 7   6 +1 7   0 +7 7   1 +6 7   5 +2 7

Lesson 1.7 Adding to 8

Add.

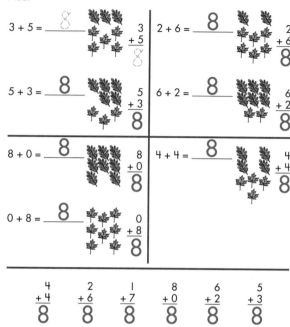

3 + 5 = 8   3 +5 8

2 + 6 = 8   2 +6 8

5 + 3 = 8   5 +3 8

6 + 2 = 8   6 +2 8

8 + 0 = 8   8 +0 8

4 + 4 = 8   4 +4 8

0 + 8 = 8   0 +8 8

4 +4 8   2 +6 8   1 +7 8   8 +0 8   6 +2 8   5 +3 8

Lesson 1.8 Adding to 9

Add.

3 + 6 = 9   3 +6 9

1 + 8 = 9   1 +8 9

6 + 3 = 9   6 +3 9

8 + 1 = 9   8 +1 9

9 + 0 = 9   9 +0 9

5 + 4 = 9   5 +4 9

0 + 9 = 9   0 +9 9

4 + 5 = 9   4 +5 9

2 + 7 = 9   2 +7 9

7 + 2 = 9   7 +2 9

4 +5 9   2 +7 9   0 +9 9   6 +3 9   7 +2 9   1 +8 9

Lesson 1.9 Adding to 10

Add.

4 + 6 = 10   4 +6 10

8 + 2 = 10   8 +2 10

6 + 4 = 10   6 +4 10

2 + 8 = 10   2 +8 10

1 + 9 = 10   1 +9 10

3 + 7 = 10   3 +7 10

9 + 1 = 10   9 +1 10

7 + 3 = 10   7 +3 10

4 +6 10   5 +5 10   10 +0 10   3 +7 10   8 +2 10   9 +1 10

Lesson 1.10 Addition Facts 7–10

Add.

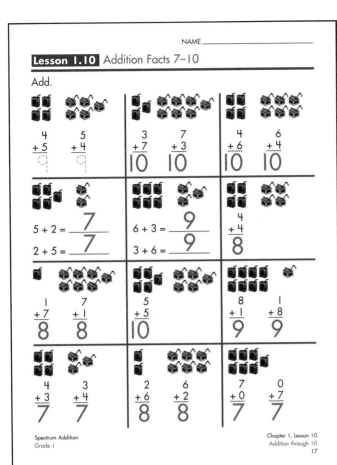

4   5
+ 5   + 4
9   9

3   7
+ 7   + 3
10   10

4   6
+ 6   + 4
10   10

5 + 2 = 7
2 + 5 = 7

6 + 3 = 9
3 + 6 = 9

4
+ 4
8

1   7
+ 7   + 1
8   8

5
+ 5
10

8   1
+ 1   + 8
9   9

4   3
+ 3   + 4
7   7

2   6
+ 6   + 2
8   8

7   0
+ 0   + 7
7   7

Lesson 1.11 Addition Practice through 10

Add.

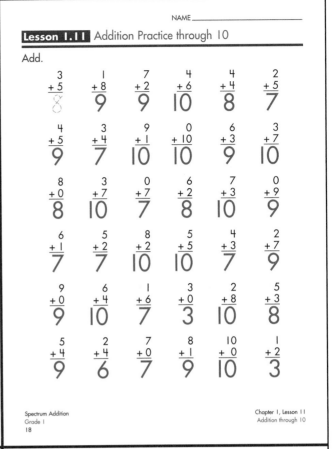

3	1	7	4	4	2
+ 5	+ 8	+ 2	+ 6	+ 4	+ 5
8	9	9	10	8	7

4	3	9	0	6	3
+ 5	+ 4	+ 1	+ 10	+ 3	+ 7
9	7	10	10	9	10

8	3	0	6	7	0
+ 0	+ 7	+ 7	+ 2	+ 3	+ 9
8	10	7	8	10	9

6	5	8	5	4	2
+ 1	+ 2	+ 2	+ 5	+ 3	+ 7
7	7	10	10	7	9

9	6	1	3	2	5
+ 0	+ 4	+ 6	+ 0	+ 8	+ 3
9	10	7	3	10	8

5	2	7	8	10	1
+ 4	+ 4	+ 0	+ 1	+ 0	+ 2
9	6	7	9	10	3

Lesson 1.12 Problem Solving

SHOW YOUR WORK

Solve each problem.

There are 8 ✈.
There are 2 ✈.
What is the sum? 10

8
+ 2
10

There are 6 🐘.
3 more 🐘 come.
What is 6 plus 3? 9

I have 4 ✏.
I buy 4 more ✏.
How many do I have now? 8

Ivan has 2 🦕.
Helen has 5 🦖.
What is 2 + 5? 7

There are 7 🦅.
3 more 🐦 come.
How many in all? 10

Lesson 1.12 Problem Solving

SHOW YOUR WORK

Solve each problem.

6 🚗 are on the ramp.
3 🚗 are on the bridge.
How many cars in all? 9

6
+ 3
9

Ines buys 1 🧸.
She buys 4 🧸.
How many toys does she buy? 5

Jordan has 3 🎈.
He has 5 🎈.
How many balloons in all? 8

3 kids drink 🧃.
2 kids drink 🧃.
What is the sum of 3 plus 2? 5

Victor used 4 ✏ in March.
He used 2 ✏ in April.
How many did he use in all? 6

Lin buys 4 🍎.
Barb buys 4 🍎.
How many fruits do they buy? 8

Spectrum Addition
Grade 1

Answer Key

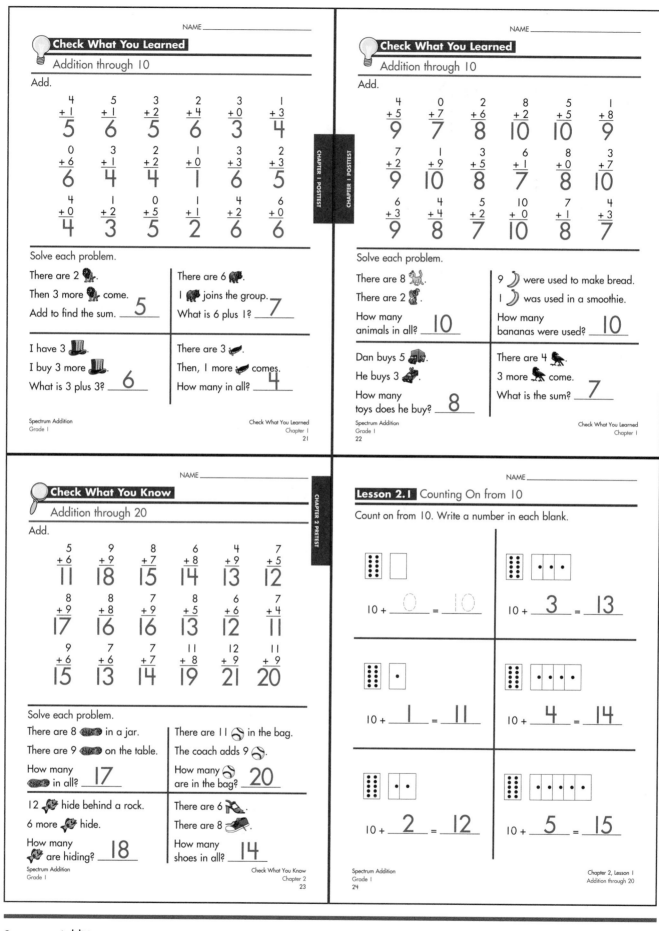

Lesson 2.1 Counting On from 10

Count on from 10. Write a number in each blank.

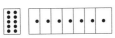 $10 + \underline{6} = \underline{16}$

  $10 + \underline{8} = \underline{18}$

$10 + \underline{7} = \underline{17}$

$10 + \underline{9} = \underline{19}$

$10 + \underline{10} = \underline{20}$

Lesson 2.2 Adding to 11

Add.

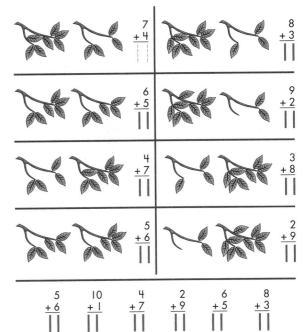

$\begin{array}{r} 7 \\ +4 \\ \hline 11 \end{array}$	$\begin{array}{r} 8 \\ +3 \\ \hline 11 \end{array}$
$\begin{array}{r} 6 \\ +5 \\ \hline 11 \end{array}$	$\begin{array}{r} 9 \\ +2 \\ \hline 11 \end{array}$
$\begin{array}{r} 4 \\ +7 \\ \hline 11 \end{array}$	$\begin{array}{r} 3 \\ +8 \\ \hline 11 \end{array}$
$\begin{array}{r} 5 \\ +6 \\ \hline 11 \end{array}$	$\begin{array}{r} 2 \\ +9 \\ \hline 11 \end{array}$

$\begin{array}{r} 5 \\ +6 \\ \hline 11 \end{array}$ $\begin{array}{r} 10 \\ +1 \\ \hline 11 \end{array}$ $\begin{array}{r} 4 \\ +7 \\ \hline 11 \end{array}$ $\begin{array}{r} 2 \\ +9 \\ \hline 11 \end{array}$ $\begin{array}{r} 6 \\ +5 \\ \hline 11 \end{array}$ $\begin{array}{r} 8 \\ +3 \\ \hline 11 \end{array}$

Lesson 2.3 Adding to 12

Add.

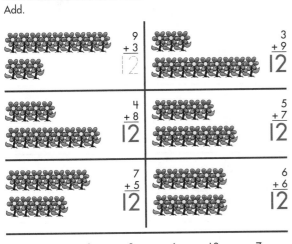

$\begin{array}{r} 9 \\ +3 \\ \hline 12 \end{array}$	$\begin{array}{r} 3 \\ +9 \\ \hline 12 \end{array}$
$\begin{array}{r} 4 \\ +8 \\ \hline 12 \end{array}$	$\begin{array}{r} 5 \\ +7 \\ \hline 12 \end{array}$
$\begin{array}{r} 7 \\ +5 \\ \hline 12 \end{array}$	$\begin{array}{r} 6 \\ +6 \\ \hline 12 \end{array}$

$\begin{array}{r} 5 \\ +7 \\ \hline 12 \end{array}$ $\begin{array}{r} 8 \\ +4 \\ \hline 12 \end{array}$ $\begin{array}{r} 9 \\ +3 \\ \hline 12 \end{array}$ $\begin{array}{r} 6 \\ +6 \\ \hline 12 \end{array}$ $\begin{array}{r} 10 \\ +2 \\ \hline 12 \end{array}$ $\begin{array}{r} 7 \\ +5 \\ \hline 12 \end{array}$

$2 + 10 = \underline{12}$ $8 + 4 = \underline{12}$ $6 + 6 = \underline{12}$

$9 + 3 = \underline{12}$ $7 + 5 = \underline{12}$ $3 + 9 = \underline{12}$

Lesson 2.4 Adding to 13

Add.

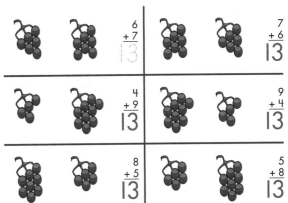

$\begin{array}{r} 6 \\ +7 \\ \hline 13 \end{array}$	$\begin{array}{r} 7 \\ +6 \\ \hline 13 \end{array}$
$\begin{array}{r} 4 \\ +9 \\ \hline 13 \end{array}$	$\begin{array}{r} 9 \\ +4 \\ \hline 13 \end{array}$
$\begin{array}{r} 8 \\ +5 \\ \hline 13 \end{array}$	$\begin{array}{r} 5 \\ +8 \\ \hline 13 \end{array}$

$\begin{array}{r} 7 \\ +6 \\ \hline 13 \end{array}$ $\begin{array}{r} 5 \\ +8 \\ \hline 13 \end{array}$ $\begin{array}{r} 9 \\ +4 \\ \hline 13 \end{array}$ $\begin{array}{r} 6 \\ +7 \\ \hline 13 \end{array}$ $\begin{array}{r} 4 \\ +9 \\ \hline 13 \end{array}$ $\begin{array}{r} 8 \\ +5 \\ \hline 13 \end{array}$

$5 + 8 = \underline{13}$ $4 + 9 = \underline{13}$ $10 + 3 = \underline{13}$

$9 + 4 = \underline{13}$ $8 + 5 = \underline{13}$ $6 + 7 = \underline{13}$

Spectrum Addition
Grade 1

Answer Key

Lesson 2.5 Adding to 14

Add.

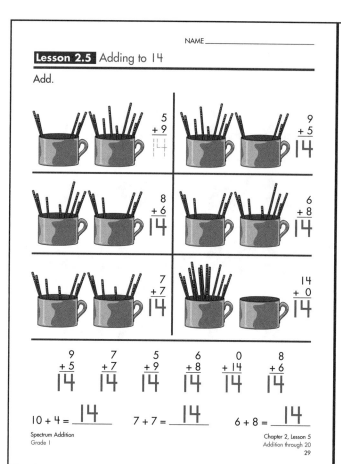

$$\begin{array}{r}5\\+9\\\hline 14\end{array}\qquad\begin{array}{r}9\\+5\\\hline 14\end{array}$$

$$\begin{array}{r}8\\+6\\\hline 14\end{array}\qquad\begin{array}{r}6\\+8\\\hline 14\end{array}$$

$$\begin{array}{r}7\\+7\\\hline 14\end{array}\qquad\begin{array}{r}14\\+0\\\hline 14\end{array}$$

$$\begin{array}{r}9\\+5\\\hline 14\end{array}\quad\begin{array}{r}7\\+7\\\hline 14\end{array}\quad\begin{array}{r}5\\+9\\\hline 14\end{array}\quad\begin{array}{r}6\\+8\\\hline 14\end{array}\quad\begin{array}{r}0\\+14\\\hline 14\end{array}\quad\begin{array}{r}8\\+6\\\hline 14\end{array}$$

$10 + 4 = \underline{14}$ $\qquad$ $7 + 7 = \underline{14}$ $\qquad$ $6 + 8 = \underline{14}$

Spectrum Addition
Grade 1

Lesson 2.6 Adding to 15

Add.

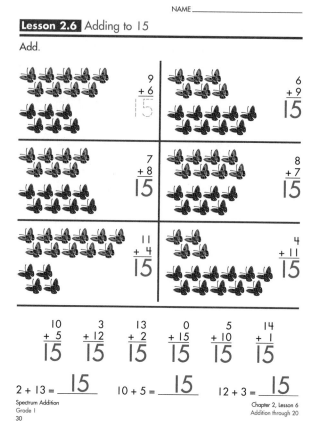

$$\begin{array}{r}9\\+6\\\hline 15\end{array}\qquad\begin{array}{r}6\\+9\\\hline 15\end{array}$$

$$\begin{array}{r}7\\+8\\\hline 15\end{array}\qquad\begin{array}{r}8\\+7\\\hline 15\end{array}$$

$$\begin{array}{r}11\\+4\\\hline 15\end{array}\qquad\begin{array}{r}4\\+11\\\hline 15\end{array}$$

$$\begin{array}{r}10\\+5\\\hline 15\end{array}\quad\begin{array}{r}3\\+12\\\hline 15\end{array}\quad\begin{array}{r}13\\+2\\\hline 15\end{array}\quad\begin{array}{r}0\\+15\\\hline 15\end{array}\quad\begin{array}{r}5\\+10\\\hline 15\end{array}\quad\begin{array}{r}14\\+1\\\hline 15\end{array}$$

$2 + 13 = \underline{15}$ $\qquad$ $10 + 5 = \underline{15}$ $\qquad$ $12 + 3 = \underline{15}$

Spectrum Addition
Grade 1

Lesson 2.7 Addition Facts 11–15

Add.

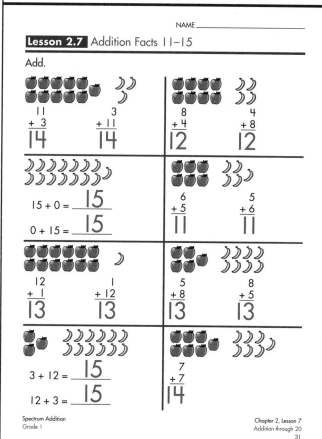

$$\begin{array}{r}11\\+3\\\hline 14\end{array}\quad\begin{array}{r}3\\+11\\\hline 14\end{array}\qquad\begin{array}{r}8\\+4\\\hline 12\end{array}\quad\begin{array}{r}4\\+8\\\hline 12\end{array}$$

$15 + 0 = \underline{15}$

$0 + 15 = \underline{15}$ $\qquad$ $\begin{array}{r}6\\+5\\\hline 11\end{array}\quad\begin{array}{r}5\\+6\\\hline 11\end{array}$

$$\begin{array}{r}12\\+1\\\hline 13\end{array}\quad\begin{array}{r}1\\+12\\\hline 13\end{array}\qquad\begin{array}{r}5\\+8\\\hline 13\end{array}\quad\begin{array}{r}8\\+5\\\hline 13\end{array}$$

$3 + 12 = \underline{15}$

$12 + 3 = \underline{15}$ $\qquad$ $\begin{array}{r}7\\+7\\\hline 14\end{array}$

Spectrum Addition
Grade 1

Lesson 2.8 Problem Solving

SHOW YOUR WORK

Solve each problem.

10 🚗 are in line.

3 more 🚗 line up.

How many 🚗 are in line? _____ 13

$$\begin{array}{r}10\\+3\\\hline 13\end{array}$$

There are 7 🍂.

There are 8 🍁.

How many leaves in all? _____ 15

There are 9 🐢 on the shelf.

There are 6 more 🐢 on the floor.

How many 🐢 in all? _____ 15

Marcus has 5 ⚾.

Sue has 7 ⚾.

What is the sum? _____ 12

Len has 6 ✈.

He has 6 🚚.

How many toys in all? _____ 12

Spectrum Addition
Grade 1

Spectrum Addition

Grade 1

84

Answer Key

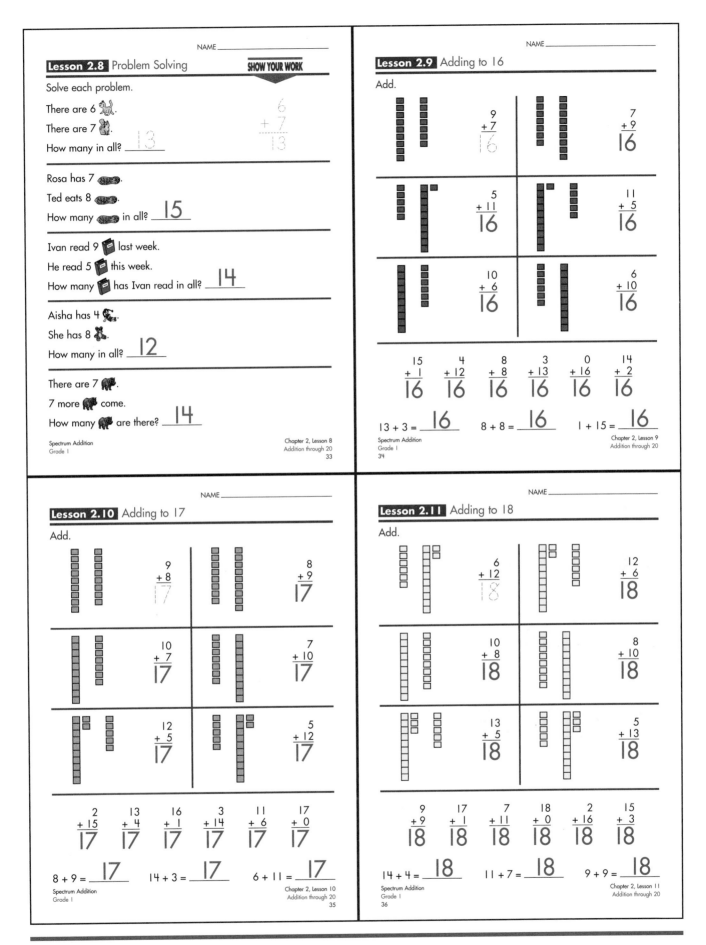

Lesson 2.8 Problem Solving

SHOW YOUR WORK

Solve each problem.

There are 6 🐱.
There are 7 🐿️.
How many in all? __13__

$$\begin{array}{r} 6 \\ + 7 \\ \hline 13 \end{array}$$

Rosa has 7 🥜.
Ted eats 8 🥜.
How many 🥜 in all? __15__

Ivan read 9 📘 last week.
He read 5 📗 this week.
How many 📘 has Ivan read in all? __14__

Aisha has 4 🧸.
She has 8 🧸.
How many in all? __12__

There are 7 🐻.
7 more 🐻 come.
How many 🐻 are there? __14__

Spectrum Addition
Grade 1

Chapter 2, Lesson 8
Addition through 20
33

Lesson 2.9 Adding to 16

Add.

$$\begin{array}{r} 9 \\ + 7 \\ \hline 16 \end{array} \qquad \begin{array}{r} 7 \\ + 9 \\ \hline 16 \end{array}$$

$$\begin{array}{r} 5 \\ + 11 \\ \hline 16 \end{array} \qquad \begin{array}{r} 11 \\ + 5 \\ \hline 16 \end{array}$$

$$\begin{array}{r} 10 \\ + 6 \\ \hline 16 \end{array} \qquad \begin{array}{r} 6 \\ + 10 \\ \hline 16 \end{array}$$

$$\begin{array}{r} 15 \\ + 1 \\ \hline 16 \end{array} \begin{array}{r} 4 \\ + 12 \\ \hline 16 \end{array} \begin{array}{r} 8 \\ + 8 \\ \hline 16 \end{array} \begin{array}{r} 3 \\ + 13 \\ \hline 16 \end{array} \begin{array}{r} 0 \\ + 16 \\ \hline 16 \end{array} \begin{array}{r} 14 \\ + 2 \\ \hline 16 \end{array}$$

13 + 3 = __16__   8 + 8 = __16__   1 + 15 = __16__

Spectrum Addition
Grade 1

Chapter 2, Lesson 9
Addition through 20
34

Lesson 2.10 Adding to 17

Add.

$$\begin{array}{r} 9 \\ + 8 \\ \hline 17 \end{array} \qquad \begin{array}{r} 8 \\ + 9 \\ \hline 17 \end{array}$$

$$\begin{array}{r} 10 \\ + 7 \\ \hline 17 \end{array} \qquad \begin{array}{r} 7 \\ + 10 \\ \hline 17 \end{array}$$

$$\begin{array}{r} 12 \\ + 5 \\ \hline 17 \end{array} \qquad \begin{array}{r} 5 \\ + 12 \\ \hline 17 \end{array}$$

$$\begin{array}{r} 2 \\ + 15 \\ \hline 17 \end{array} \begin{array}{r} 13 \\ + 4 \\ \hline 17 \end{array} \begin{array}{r} 16 \\ + 1 \\ \hline 17 \end{array} \begin{array}{r} 3 \\ + 14 \\ \hline 17 \end{array} \begin{array}{r} 11 \\ + 6 \\ \hline 17 \end{array} \begin{array}{r} 17 \\ + 0 \\ \hline 17 \end{array}$$

8 + 9 = __17__   14 + 3 = __17__   6 + 11 = __17__

Spectrum Addition
Grade 1

Chapter 2, Lesson 10
Addition through 20
35

Lesson 2.11 Adding to 18

Add.

$$\begin{array}{r} 6 \\ + 12 \\ \hline 18 \end{array} \qquad \begin{array}{r} 12 \\ + 6 \\ \hline 18 \end{array}$$

$$\begin{array}{r} 10 \\ + 8 \\ \hline 18 \end{array} \qquad \begin{array}{r} 8 \\ + 10 \\ \hline 18 \end{array}$$

$$\begin{array}{r} 13 \\ + 5 \\ \hline 18 \end{array} \qquad \begin{array}{r} 5 \\ + 13 \\ \hline 18 \end{array}$$

$$\begin{array}{r} 9 \\ + 9 \\ \hline 18 \end{array} \begin{array}{r} 17 \\ + 1 \\ \hline 18 \end{array} \begin{array}{r} 7 \\ + 11 \\ \hline 18 \end{array} \begin{array}{r} 18 \\ + 0 \\ \hline 18 \end{array} \begin{array}{r} 2 \\ + 16 \\ \hline 18 \end{array} \begin{array}{r} 15 \\ + 3 \\ \hline 18 \end{array}$$

14 + 4 = __18__   11 + 7 = __18__   9 + 9 = __18__

Spectrum Addition
Grade 1

Chapter 2, Lesson 11
Addition through 20
36

Spectrum Addition
Grade 1

Answer Key

Lesson 2.12 Adding to 19

Add.

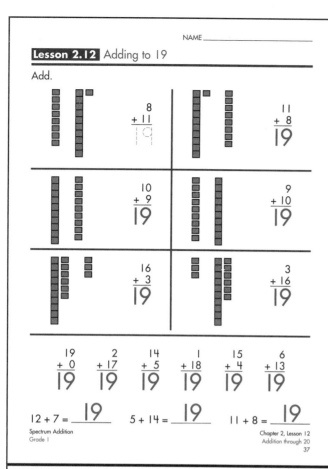

$$\begin{array}{r} 8 \\ +11 \\ \hline 19 \end{array} \qquad \begin{array}{r} 11 \\ +8 \\ \hline 19 \end{array}$$

$$\begin{array}{r} 10 \\ +9 \\ \hline 19 \end{array} \qquad \begin{array}{r} 9 \\ +10 \\ \hline 19 \end{array}$$

$$\begin{array}{r} 16 \\ +3 \\ \hline 19 \end{array} \qquad \begin{array}{r} 3 \\ +16 \\ \hline 19 \end{array}$$

$$\begin{array}{r} 19 \\ +0 \\ \hline 19 \end{array} \quad \begin{array}{r} 2 \\ +17 \\ \hline 19 \end{array} \quad \begin{array}{r} 14 \\ +5 \\ \hline 19 \end{array} \quad \begin{array}{r} 1 \\ +18 \\ \hline 19 \end{array} \quad \begin{array}{r} 15 \\ +4 \\ \hline 19 \end{array} \quad \begin{array}{r} 6 \\ +13 \\ \hline 19 \end{array}$$

$12 + 7 = \underline{19}$ \qquad $5 + 14 = \underline{19}$ \qquad $11 + 8 = \underline{19}$

Chapter 2, Lesson 12
Addition through 20

Lesson 2.13 Adding to 20

Add.

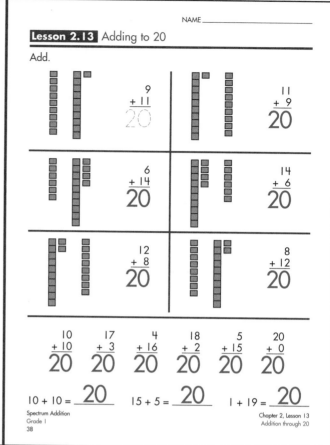

$$\begin{array}{r} 9 \\ +11 \\ \hline 20 \end{array} \qquad \begin{array}{r} 11 \\ +9 \\ \hline 20 \end{array}$$

$$\begin{array}{r} 6 \\ +14 \\ \hline 20 \end{array} \qquad \begin{array}{r} 14 \\ +6 \\ \hline 20 \end{array}$$

$$\begin{array}{r} 12 \\ +8 \\ \hline 20 \end{array} \qquad \begin{array}{r} 8 \\ +12 \\ \hline 20 \end{array}$$

$$\begin{array}{r} 10 \\ +10 \\ \hline 20 \end{array} \quad \begin{array}{r} 17 \\ +3 \\ \hline 20 \end{array} \quad \begin{array}{r} 4 \\ +16 \\ \hline 20 \end{array} \quad \begin{array}{r} 18 \\ +2 \\ \hline 20 \end{array} \quad \begin{array}{r} 5 \\ +15 \\ \hline 20 \end{array} \quad \begin{array}{r} 20 \\ +0 \\ \hline 20 \end{array}$$

$10 + 10 = \underline{20}$ \qquad $15 + 5 = \underline{20}$ \qquad $1 + 19 = \underline{20}$

Chapter 2, Lesson 13
Addition through 20

Lesson 2.14 Addition Facts 16–20

Add.

$$\begin{array}{r} 14 \\ +3 \\ \hline 17 \end{array} \qquad \begin{array}{r} 3 \\ +14 \\ \hline 17 \end{array} \qquad \begin{array}{r} 5 \\ +13 \\ \hline 18 \end{array} \qquad \begin{array}{r} 13 \\ +5 \\ \hline 18 \end{array}$$

$2 + 16 = \underline{18}$
$16 + 2 = \underline{18}$

$$\begin{array}{r} 14 \\ +6 \\ \hline 20 \end{array} \qquad \begin{array}{r} 6 \\ +14 \\ \hline 20 \end{array}$$

$$\begin{array}{r} 18 \\ +1 \\ \hline 19 \end{array} \qquad \begin{array}{r} 1 \\ +18 \\ \hline 19 \end{array} \qquad \begin{array}{r} 7 \\ +10 \\ \hline 17 \end{array} \qquad \begin{array}{r} 10 \\ +7 \\ \hline 17 \end{array}$$

$16 + 4 = \underline{20}$
$4 + 16 = \underline{20}$

$$\begin{array}{r} 8 \\ +8 \\ \hline 16 \end{array}$$

Chapter 2, Lesson 14
Addition through 20

Lesson 2.15 Addition Practice through 20

Add.

$$\begin{array}{r} 7 \\ +9 \\ \hline 16 \end{array} \quad \begin{array}{r} 8 \\ +3 \\ \hline 11 \end{array} \quad \begin{array}{r} 7 \\ +8 \\ \hline 15 \end{array} \quad \begin{array}{r} 18 \\ +1 \\ \hline 19 \end{array} \quad \begin{array}{r} 8 \\ +4 \\ \hline 12 \end{array} \quad \begin{array}{r} 9 \\ +8 \\ \hline 17 \end{array}$$

$$\begin{array}{r} 7 \\ +6 \\ \hline 13 \end{array} \quad \begin{array}{r} 5 \\ +9 \\ \hline 14 \end{array} \quad \begin{array}{r} 8 \\ +8 \\ \hline 16 \end{array} \quad \begin{array}{r} 17 \\ +3 \\ \hline 20 \end{array} \quad \begin{array}{r} 9 \\ +4 \\ \hline 13 \end{array} \quad \begin{array}{r} 3 \\ +8 \\ \hline 11 \end{array}$$

$$\begin{array}{r} 2 \\ +10 \\ \hline 12 \end{array} \quad \begin{array}{r} 7 \\ +5 \\ \hline 12 \end{array} \quad \begin{array}{r} 3 \\ +17 \\ \hline 20 \end{array} \quad \begin{array}{r} 12 \\ +8 \\ \hline 20 \end{array} \quad \begin{array}{r} 15 \\ +5 \\ \hline 20 \end{array} \quad \begin{array}{r} 9 \\ +9 \\ \hline 18 \end{array}$$

$$\begin{array}{r} 14 \\ +5 \\ \hline 19 \end{array} \quad \begin{array}{r} 1 \\ +16 \\ \hline 17 \end{array} \quad \begin{array}{r} 3 \\ +9 \\ \hline 12 \end{array} \quad \begin{array}{r} 18 \\ +2 \\ \hline 20 \end{array} \quad \begin{array}{r} 6 \\ +6 \\ \hline 12 \end{array} \quad \begin{array}{r} 0 \\ +14 \\ \hline 14 \end{array}$$

$$\begin{array}{r} 16 \\ +3 \\ \hline 19 \end{array} \quad \begin{array}{r} 7 \\ +7 \\ \hline 14 \end{array} \quad \begin{array}{r} 6 \\ +8 \\ \hline 14 \end{array} \quad \begin{array}{r} 4 \\ +9 \\ \hline 13 \end{array} \quad \begin{array}{r} 12 \\ +6 \\ \hline 18 \end{array} \quad \begin{array}{r} 5 \\ +15 \\ \hline 20 \end{array}$$

$$\begin{array}{r} 10 \\ +10 \\ \hline 20 \end{array} \quad \begin{array}{r} 17 \\ +2 \\ \hline 19 \end{array} \quad \begin{array}{r} 11 \\ +6 \\ \hline 17 \end{array} \quad \begin{array}{r} 10 \\ +0 \\ \hline 10 \end{array} \quad \begin{array}{r} 14 \\ +1 \\ \hline 15 \end{array} \quad \begin{array}{r} 2 \\ +18 \\ \hline 20 \end{array}$$

Chapter 2, Lesson 15
Addition through 20

Answer Key

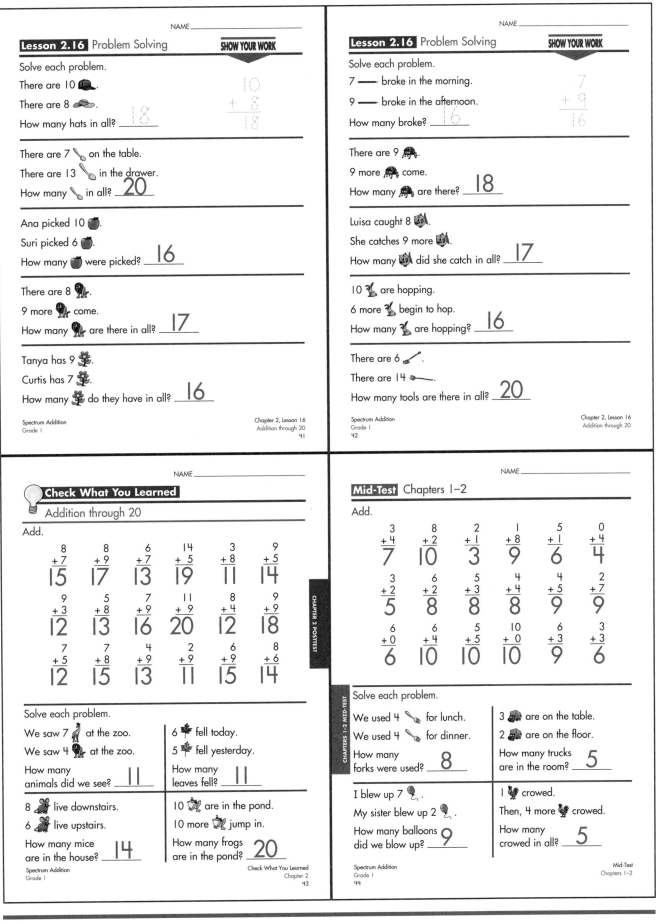

Page 45

Mid-Test Chapters 1–2

SHOW YOUR WORK

Add.

```
  7      3      7     18      8      9
+ 9    + 8    + 8    + 1    + 4    + 8
 16     11     15     19     12     17

 12      5     17      5      4      9
+ 6    + 9    + 3    + 7    + 7    + 9
 18     14     20     12     11     18

  6     10     12      8      5     14
+ 7    + 5    + 8    + 5    + 6    + 5
 13     15     20     13     11     19
```

Solve each problem.

10 🐟 are in the tank.
4 🐟 are in the tank.
How many fish are in the tank? __14__

One bowl has 6 🍎.
Another bowl has 5 🍎.
What is the sum? __11__

The candy shop sold 12 🍭 on Monday.
The shop sold 8 🍭 on Tuesday.
How many 🍭 have sold so far this week? __20__

7 🐐 stood on the cliff.
8 🐐 stood under the cliff.
How many goats in all? __15__

Spectrum Addition
Grade 1

Mid-Test
Chapters 1–2
45

Page 46

Check What You Know

Addition Equations and Strategies

Write a number to complete each equation.

$16 + 2 = \boxed{18}$	$\boxed{8} + 3 = 11$	$7 + 3 = \boxed{3} + 7$
$8 + 2 = 5 + \boxed{5}$	$9 + 5 = 5 + \boxed{9}$	$11 + 3 = \boxed{7} + 7$
$20 = \boxed{20}$	$6 + \boxed{9} = 8 + 7$	$4 + 6 = 10 + \boxed{0}$

Write any numbers in the blanks to make the equations correct.

$8 + 4 = \boxed{} + \boxed{}$
Answers will vary.

$\boxed{} + \boxed{} = 2 + 3$
Answers will vary.

Circle equations that are true. Draw an X on equations that are not true.

```
 18          8         14          3
+ 2        + 2        + 6        + 8
 20         18         20         11
 ✗          ✗       (circled)   (circled)
```

Spectrum Addition
Grade 1
46

Check What You Know
Chapter 3

Page 47

Check What You Know

Addition Equations and Strategies

Add by counting on.

How many is 4 more than 8 🐞? __12__

What is 6 more than 4 🍁? __10__

Think about how to make each equation easier to solve. Write a number in the blank.

$7 + 5 =$ $2 + 5 + 5 =$ $2 + \boxed{10} = 12$

$6 + 7 =$ $6 + 6 + 1 =$ $12 + \boxed{1} = 13$

Add.

```
  8      9     12      3
  2      5      3      8
+ 4    + 5    + 2    + 1
 14     19     17     12
```

Spectrum Addition
Grade 1

Check What You Know
Chapter 3
47

Page 48

Lesson 3.1 Addition Equations

In an equation, the numbers before the equal sign (=) are equal to the numbers after the equal sign.

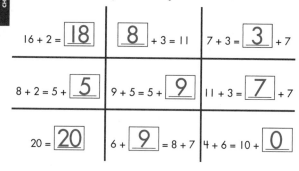

$$\begin{array}{r} 2 \\ + 4 \\ \hline 6 \end{array} \Big\}$$

An equation like this uses a line instead of an equal sign. The line means "equal to."

Write a number to complete each equation.

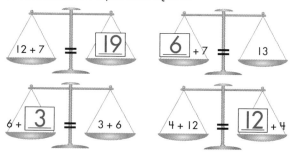

Spectrum Addition
Grade 1
48

Chapter 3, Lesson 1
Addition Equations and Strategies

Spectrum Addition

Grade 1

88

Answer Key

NAME

Lesson 3.1 Addition Equations

Write a number to complete each equation.

 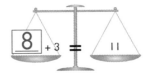

$5 + \boxed{5} = 10$ $\boxed{8} + 3 = 11$

$4 + 3 = \boxed{7}$	$2 + 6 = 6 + \boxed{2}$	$\boxed{3} + 12 = 12 + 3$
$8 + \boxed{8} = 16$	$4 + 3 = \boxed{3} + 4$	$0 + 4 = 4 + \boxed{0}$
$\boxed{19} + 1 = 20$	$10 + \boxed{1} = 1 + 10$	$9 + \boxed{5} = 5 + 9$
$13 + \boxed{6} = 19$	$\boxed{8} + 7 = 7 + 8$	$5 + 10 = 10 + \boxed{5}$

NAME

Lesson 3.2 Completing Equations

The numbers before and after the equal sign may look the same or different. As long as they are equal, the equation is correct.

$4 = 4$ $2 + 2 = 4 + 0$

$4 = 3 + 1$ $1 + 3 = 2 + 2$

Write a number to complete each equation.

$8 = \boxed{8}$	$10 = 4 + \boxed{6}$	$0 + 5 = 5 + \boxed{0}$
$5 + 2 = \boxed{2} + 5$	$6 + 2 = 4 + \boxed{4}$	$14 + 4 = 9 + \boxed{9}$
$15 + 5 = \boxed{20}$	$4 + 9 = \boxed{10} + 3$	$3 + \boxed{2} = 3 + 1 + 1$

NAME

Lesson 3.2 Completing Equations

Write any numbers in the blanks to make each equation correct.

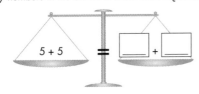

$5 + 5 = \boxed{} + \boxed{}$

Answers will vary.

$\boxed{\ } + \boxed{\ } = 6 + 2$	$0 + 8 = \boxed{\ } + \boxed{\ }$
$9 + 5 = \boxed{\ } + \boxed{\ }$	$\boxed{\ } + \boxed{\ } = 6 + 3$
$\boxed{\ } + \boxed{\ } = 7 + 3$	$14 + 2 = \boxed{\ } + \boxed{\ }$
$17 + 3 = \boxed{\ } + \boxed{\ }$	$\boxed{\ } + \boxed{\ } = 4 + 3$
$\boxed{\ } + \boxed{\ } = 11 + 4$	$3 + 3 = \boxed{\ } + \boxed{\ }$

NAME

Lesson 3.3 Completing Equation Pairs

Write the same number to complete each pair of equations.

$\begin{array}{r} 14 \\ + \boxed{6} \\ \hline 20 \end{array}$	$\begin{array}{r} \boxed{6} \\ + 4 \\ \hline 10 \end{array}$	$\begin{array}{r} 5 \\ + \boxed{8} \\ \hline 13 \end{array}$	$\begin{array}{r} \boxed{8} \\ + 12 \\ \hline 20 \end{array}$
$\begin{array}{r} \boxed{15} \\ + 3 \\ \hline 18 \end{array}$	$\begin{array}{r} 10 \\ + 5 \\ \hline \boxed{15} \end{array}$	$\begin{array}{r} 16 \\ + \boxed{0} \\ \hline 16 \end{array}$	$\begin{array}{r} \boxed{0} \\ + 3 \\ \hline 3 \end{array}$
$\begin{array}{r} 9 \\ + \boxed{2} \\ \hline 11 \end{array}$	$\begin{array}{r} 0 \\ + \boxed{2} \\ \hline 2 \end{array}$	$\begin{array}{r} 16 \\ + 3 \\ \hline \boxed{19} \end{array}$	$\begin{array}{r} \boxed{19} \\ + 1 \\ \hline 20 \end{array}$
$\begin{array}{r} \boxed{12} \\ + 3 \\ \hline 15 \end{array}$	$\begin{array}{r} 8 \\ + 4 \\ \hline \boxed{12} \end{array}$	$\begin{array}{r} \boxed{7} \\ + 7 \\ \hline 14 \end{array}$	$\begin{array}{r} 8 \\ + \boxed{7} \\ \hline 15 \end{array}$

Lesson 3.4 Evaluating Equations

If the numbers before the equal sign (=) do not equal the numbers after the equal sign, the equation is not true.

Circle each equation that is true. Draw an X through each equation that is not true.

$\boxed{10 + 7 = 17}$	$8 + 6 = 16$ ✗	$12 + 3 = 12 + 2 + 2$ ✗
$\boxed{8 + 2 = 5 + 5}$	$\boxed{5 + 9 = 9 + 5}$	$4 + 7 = 12$ ✗
$\begin{array}{r} 10 \\ + \\ \hline 11 \end{array}$ ✗	$\boxed{\begin{array}{r} 8 \\ + 6 \\ \hline 14 \end{array}}$	$\boxed{\begin{array}{r} 9 \\ + 9 \\ \hline 18 \end{array}}$
$\begin{array}{r} 0 \\ + \\ \hline 11 \end{array}$ ✗	$\boxed{\begin{array}{r} 5 \\ + 3 \\ \hline 8 \end{array}}$	$\begin{array}{r} 17 \\ + 2 \\ \hline 20 \end{array}$ ✗

Chapter 3, Lesson 4
Addition Equations and Strategies

Lesson 3.5 Counting On

SHOW YOUR WORK

One way to add to a number is to count ahead.

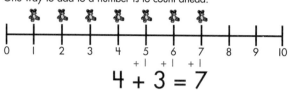

$$4 + 3 = 7$$

Add by counting on.

How many is 2 more than 7 🐭? ___ 9 $7 + 2 = 9$

What is 1 more than 8 🐶? ___ 9

How many is 1 more than 9 🦋? ___ 10

What is 3 more than 16 🐐? ___ 19

There are 4 more than 13 🐕. How many 🐕 are there? ___ 17

How many is 5 more than 12 🌼? ___ 17

Chapter 3, Lesson 5
Addition Equations and Strategies

Lesson 3.6 Doubles and Near-Doubles

Add to find the sum.

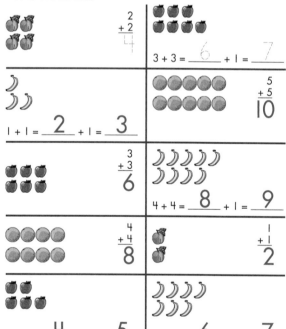

$\begin{array}{r} 2 \\ + 2 \\ \hline 4 \end{array}$

$3 + 3 = \underline{6} + 1 = \underline{7}$

$1 + 1 = \underline{2} + 1 = \underline{3}$

$\begin{array}{r} 5 \\ + 5 \\ \hline 10 \end{array}$

$\begin{array}{r} 3 \\ + 3 \\ \hline 6 \end{array}$

$4 + 4 = \underline{8} + 1 = \underline{9}$

$\begin{array}{r} 4 \\ + 4 \\ \hline 8 \end{array}$

$\begin{array}{r} 1 \\ + 1 \\ \hline 2 \end{array}$

$2 + 2 = \underline{4} + 1 = \underline{5}$ $3 + 3 = \underline{6} + 1 = \underline{7}$

Chapter 3, Lesson 6
Addition Equations and Strategies

Lesson 3.7 Making 10

One way to add is to think about what equals 10.

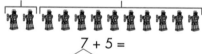

$$7 + 5 =$$
$$2 + 5 + 5 =$$
$$2 + 10 = 12$$

Write a number in each blank. Think about what equals 10.

$8 + 6 =$ $8 + 2 + 4 =$ $10 + \boxed{4} = 14$

$7 + 6 =$ $7 + 3 + 3 =$ $10 + \boxed{3} = 13$

Chapter 3, Lesson 7
Addition Equations and Strategies

Answer Key

Lesson 3.8 Making Known Sums

One way to add is to think about equations (like doubles) that are easy to solve.

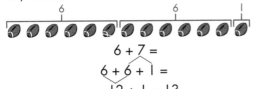

$$6 + 7 =$$
$$6 + 6 + 1 =$$
$$12 + 1 = 13$$

Write a number in each blank. Think about what equals 10.

5 + 6 =   5 + 5 + 1 = $10 + \boxed{1} = 11$

7 + 8 =   7 + 7 + 1 = $14 + \boxed{1} = 15$

Spectrum Addition
Grade 1

Chapter 3, Lesson 8
Addition Equations and Strategies
57

Lesson 3.9 Adding 3 Numbers

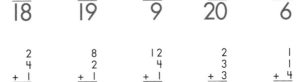

	Add the ones.	Add the tens.
12	12	12
4	4	4
+ 3	+ 3	+ 3
	9	sum = 19

Add.

10	11	4	15	2
5	3	3	3	2
+ 3	+ 5	+ 2	+ 2	+ 2
18	19	9	20	6

2	8	12	2	1
4	2	4	3	1
+ 1	+ 1	+ 1	+ 3	+ 4
7	11	17	8	6

5	15	13	11	12
4	1	2	6	2
+ 1	+ 1	+ 1	+ 2	+ 6
10	17	16	19	20

Spectrum Addition
Grade 1
58

Chapter 3, Lesson 9
Addition Equations and Strategies

Lesson 3.10 Making 10 to Add 3 Numbers

When you add three numbers, look for two numbers that equal ten. Rewrite to make the equation easier to solve.

$$+ 8 \quad + 8$$
$$18 \quad 18$$

Look at each pair of equations. In the first equation, circle two numbers that equal 10. Write the missing number in the second equation.

5	10	4	10
5	+ $\boxed{7}$	6	+ $\boxed{9}$
+ 7		+ 9	
17	17	19	19

6	6	5	$\boxed{5}$
2	+ $\boxed{10}$	8	
+ 8		+ 2	+ 10
16	16	15	15

9	10	6	6
1	+ $\boxed{2}$	9	+ $\boxed{10}$
+ 2		+ 1	
12	12	16	16

Spectrum Addition
Grade 1

Chapter 3, Lesson 10
Addition Equations and Strategies
59

Lesson 3.11 Problem Solving   SHOW YOUR WORK

Solve each problem.

Lanie has 10 🐕.
Tina has 2 🐕. Paul has 5 🐕.
How many 🐕 do they have in all? __17__

$$10$$
$$2$$
$$+ 5$$
$$17$$

The toy store sold 7 🎎 in March,
3 🎎 in April, and 8 🎎 in May.
How many 🎎 did the toy store sell in all? __18__

Felicia puts 2 🚂, 2 🧸, and
8 🚗 on shelves. How many
toys does Felicia put on shelves? __12__

The toy store has 8 🚗, 2 🚚,
and 10 🚙. How many of these
toys does the toy store have in all? __20__

The bakery sells 4 🧁 on Monday, 10 🧁
on Tuesday, and 6 🧁 on Wednesday.
How many 🧁 did the bakery sell? __20__

Spectrum Addition
Grade 1
60

Chapter 3, Lesson 11
Addition Equations and Strategies

Spectrum Addition
Grade 1

Answer Key

💡 Check What You Learned

Addition Equations and Strategies

Write a number to complete each equation.

$11 + 3 = \boxed{14}$ | $9 + 1 = \boxed{1} + 9$ | $7 + 5 = 6 + \boxed{6}$

$14 + 4 = \boxed{11} + 7$ | $9 + \boxed{7} = 5 + 11$ | $12 + 3 = 8 + \boxed{7}$

Write any numbers in the blanks to make the equations correct.

$12 + 3 = \underline{} + \underline{}$ $\underline{} + \underline{} = 0 + 8$

Answers will vary.   Answers will vary.

Write the same number to complete each pair of equations.

$\boxed{10}$ 2 3 4
$+\ 4$ $+\boxed{10}$ $+\boxed{8}$ $+\ 4$
$\overline{14}$ $\overline{12}$ $\overline{11}$ $\boxed{8}$

Circle equations that are true. Draw an X on equations that are not true.

($6 + 12 = 18$)   ✗ $10 + 3 + 6 = 20$ ✗   ✗ $9 + 7 = 17$ ✗   ($4 + 3 + 1 = 8$)

💡 Check What You Learned

Addition Equations and Strategies

Add by counting on.

How many is 6 more than 5 🐢? $\underline{11}$

Think about how to make each equation easier to solve. Write a number in the blank.

$8 + 3 =$ $8 + 2 + 1 =$ $10 + \boxed{1} = 11$

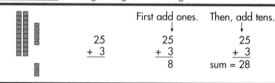

$7 + 8 =$ $7 + 7 + 1 =$ $\boxed{14} + 1 = 15$

Add.

5 11 2 1
5 6 9 7
$+\ 8$ $+\ 2$ $+\ 4$ $+\ 3$
$\overline{18}$ $\overline{19}$ $\overline{15}$ $\overline{11}$

On the table, there are 10 🥄, 3 🥛, and 5 🥣. How many things are on the table? $\underline{18}$

🔍 Check What You Know

Addition through 100

Add.

37 43 81 23 56
$+\ 2$ $+\ 5$ $+\ 4$ $+\ 1$ $+\ 2$
$\overline{39}$ $\overline{48}$ $\overline{85}$ $\overline{24}$ $\overline{58}$

44 77 69 19 46
$+\ 6$ $+\ 3$ $+\ 2$ $+\ 3$ $+\ 4$
$\overline{50}$ $\overline{80}$ $\overline{71}$ $\overline{22}$ $\overline{50}$

14 39 42 21 18
$+10$ $+20$ $+30$ $+40$ $+30$
$\overline{24}$ $\overline{59}$ $\overline{72}$ $\overline{61}$ $\overline{48}$

55 82 62 11 22
$+40$ $+10$ $+30$ $+80$ $+60$
$\overline{95}$ $\overline{92}$ $\overline{92}$ $\overline{91}$ $\overline{82}$

Write a number to answer each question.

What is 10 more than 16? $\underline{26}$

What is 10 more than 65? $\underline{75}$

What is 10 more than 78? $\underline{88}$

What is 10 more than 46? $\underline{56}$

Lesson 4.1 Adding 2-Digit and 1-Digit Numbers

First add ones.   Then, add tens.

25 25 25
$+\ 3$ $+\ 3$ $+\ 3$
           $\overline{\ 8}$ sum = 28

Add the ones.	Put the ones in the ones place. Put the ten in the tens place.	Add the tens.
38 8 $+4$ $+4$? $\overline{12}$ 12 = 1 ten and 2 ones	$\overset{1}{38}$ $+\ 4$ $\overline{\ 2}$	$\overset{1}{38}$ $+\ 4$ sum = 42

Add.

15 19 27 20 13
$+\ 2$ $+\ 6$ $+\ 5$ $+\ 6$ $+\ 4$
$\overline{17}$ $\overline{25}$ $\overline{32}$ $\overline{26}$ $\overline{17}$

38 22 29 47 14
$+\ 8$ $+\ 6$ $+\ 3$ $+\ 2$ $+\ 1$
$\overline{46}$ $\overline{28}$ $\overline{32}$ $\overline{49}$ $\overline{15}$

63 53 87 41 79
$+\ 5$ $+\ 6$ $+\ 2$ $+\ 4$ $+\ 9$
$\overline{68}$ $\overline{59}$ $\overline{89}$ $\overline{45}$ $\overline{88}$

Lesson 4.1 Adding 2-Digit and 1-Digit Numbers

Add.

63 + 6 **69**	42 + 5 **47**	29 + 9 **38**	71 + 8 **79**	62 + 3 **65**
45 + 4 **49**	19 + 6 **25**	30 + 9 **39**	16 + 7 **23**	22 + 4 **26**
30 + 6 **36**	81 + 7 **88**	47 + 2 **49**	56 + 5 **61**	48 + 7 **55**
15 + 8 **23**	67 + 1 **68**	42 + 3 **45**	56 + 4 **60**	39 + 5 **44**
23 + 8 **31**	17 + 7 **24**	44 + 6 **50**	16 + 3 **19**	86 + 6 **92**
90 + 4 **94**	31 + 9 **40**	68 + 4 **72**	24 + 5 **29**	36 + 8 **44**

Lesson 4.2 Adding Multiples of 10 to 2-Digit Numbers

6 tens and 8 ones plus 2 tens equals 8 tens and 8 ones.

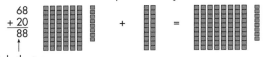

68
 + 20
 88

Only the tens place changes.

Use the pictures to help you add.

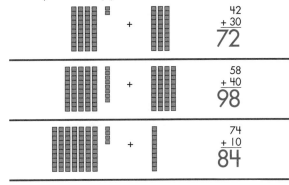

(picture) + (picture)	42 + 30 **72**
(picture) + (picture)	58 + 40 **98**
(picture) + (picture)	74 + 10 **84**

Lesson 4.2 Adding Multiples of 10 to 2-Digit Numbers

Add.

15 + 10 **25**	19 + 20 **39**	23 + 20 **43**	31 + 10 **41**	47 + 20 **67**
13 + 30 **43**	29 + 40 **69**	17 + 40 **57**	11 + 50 **61**	60 + 30 **90**
75 + 10 **85**	50 + 40 **90**	25 + 70 **95**	42 + 50 **92**	12 + 80 **92**
18 + 20 **38**	12 + 80 **92**	20 + 40 **60**	59 + 20 **79**	15 + 70 **85**
17 + 40 **57**	11 + 20 **31**	49 + 30 **79**	86 + 10 **96**	25 + 70 **95**
25 + 30 **55**	63 + 20 **83**	18 + 50 **68**	46 + 40 **86**	72 + 20 **92**

Lesson 4.3 Adding 10 Mentally

Add 10 to each number. Solve the problem only in your mind. Write the number in the thought bubble.

+10 **48**
 38

+10 **74**
 64

+10 **23**
 13

+10 **66**
 56

+10 **97**
 87

+10 **64**
 54

+10 **21**
 11

+10 **100**
 90

+10 **36**
 26

+10 **18**
 8

+10 **12**
 2

+10 **53**
 43

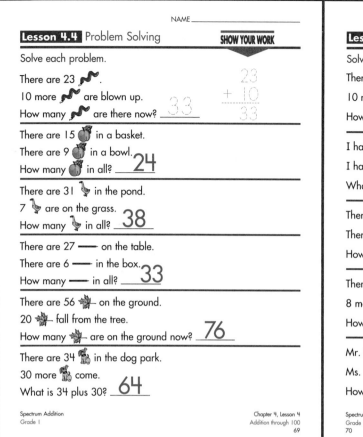

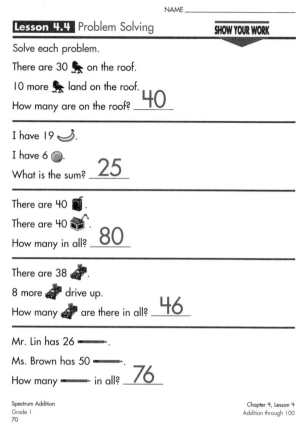

Top Left Panel

Lesson 4.4 Problem Solving | SHOW YOUR WORK

Solve each problem.

There are 23 🐛.
10 more 🐛 are blown up.
How many 🐛 are there now? __33__

$$\begin{array}{r} 23 \\ + 10 \\ \hline 33 \end{array}$$

There are 15 🧅 in a basket.
There are 9 🧅 in a bowl.
How many 🧅 in all? __24__

There are 31 🦢 in the pond.
7 🦢 are on the grass.
How many 🦢 in all? __38__

There are 27 — on the table.
There are 6 — in the box.
How many — in all? __33__

There are 56 🍁 on the ground.
20 🍁 fall from the tree.
How many 🍁 are on the ground now? __76__

There are 34 🐕 in the dog park.
30 more 🐕 come.
What is 34 plus 30? __64__

Spectrum Addition
Grade 1

Chapter 4, Lesson 4
Addition through 100
69

Top Right Panel

Lesson 4.4 Problem Solving | SHOW YOUR WORK

Solve each problem.

There are 30 🦅 on the roof.
10 more 🦅 land on the roof.
How many are on the roof? __40__

I have 19 🍌.
I have 6 ⚫.
What is the sum? __25__

There are 40 📦.
There are 40 📦.
How many in all? __80__

There are 38 🚗.
8 more 🚗 drive up.
How many 🚗 are there in all? __46__

Mr. Lin has 26 ━━.
Ms. Brown has 50 ━━.
How many ━━ in all? __76__

Spectrum Addition
Grade 1
70

Chapter 4, Lesson 4
Addition through 100

Bottom Left Panel

Lesson 4.5 Addition Practice through 100

Add.

9 +8 = 17	9 +7 = 16	16 +9 = 25	27 +8 = 35	28 +5 = 33	37 +7 = 44
49 +9 = 58	67 +9 = 76	58 +7 = 65	18 +9 = 27	78 +6 = 84	96 +4 = 100
87 +6 = 93	29 +5 = 34	79 +6 = 85	8 +8 = 16	46 +8 = 54	66 +7 = 73
36 +10 = 46	15 +10 = 25	78 +10 = 88	89 +10 = 99	9 +10 = 19	47 +10 = 57
22 +40 = 62	63 +30 = 93	35 +50 = 85	71 +20 = 91	27 +30 = 57	43 +40 = 83
59 +20 = 79	80 +10 = 90	16 +40 = 56	12 +70 = 82	13 +60 = 73	17 +80 = 97

Spectrum Addition
Grade 1

Chapter 4, Lesson 5
Addition through 100
71

Bottom Right Panel

CHAPTER 4 POSTTEST

💡 **Check What You Learned**

Addition through 100

Add.

12 +4 = 16	18 +2 = 20	15 +3 = 18	17 +1 = 18	13 +6 = 19
35 +7 = 42	48 +1 = 49	56 +6 = 62	79 +2 = 81	22 +6 = 28
83 +10 = 93	14 +10 = 24	36 +10 = 46	41 +10 = 51	90 +10 = 100
54 +10 = 64	10 +10 = 20	17 +10 = 27	25 +10 = 35	67 +10 = 77
27 +20 = 47	33 +30 = 63	48 +30 = 78	62 +20 = 82	19 +40 = 59
50 +20 = 70	62 +10 = 72	49 +20 = 69	38 +40 = 78	11 +60 = 71

Spectrum Addition
Grade 1
72

Check What You Learned
Chapter 4

Spectrum Addition

Grade 1

94

Answer Key

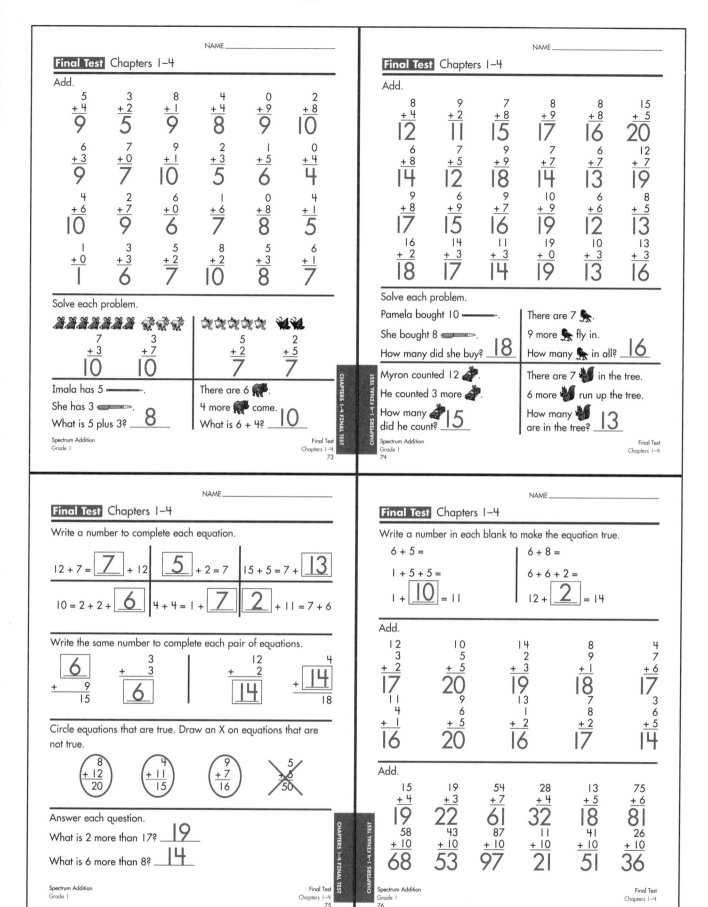